GW00738347

POPULAR REWARDS

Redbeard and the
Enchanted Tree

and other stories

Award Publications Limited

*With thanks to Elizabeth Dale,
Jenny Jinks, Lizzie Strong and
Marjorie-Ann Gladman*

ISBN 978-1-78270-349-5

First published 2023

Published by Award Publications Limited,
The Old Riding School, Welbeck,
Worksop, S80 3LR

**𝐎 /awardpublications 𝐎 @award.books 𝐘 @award_books
www.awardpublications.co.uk**

23-1053 1

Printed in China

Contents

Redbeard and the Enchanted Tree

Redbeard is a very hard-working carpenter, who lives all by himself in the log cabin he has built in the middle of a great forest. Everyone who knows him likes him. He is poor but he is kind-hearted and always willing to help. His days are spent making beautiful furniture or exquisitely carved statues of the animals and birds that live in the forest. Redbeard loves the forest so much that he only ever uses fallen trees he finds on the forest floor.

Each morning, he marches cheerfully into the forest, whistling to the birds as they chorus back and calling 'Good day!' to anyone he meets. Redbeard truly is a most warm-hearted fellow.

However, as all people do, even Redbeard has a flaw. He is vain and so very proud of his grand beard – it is his pride and joy. Every evening, before he gets into bed, he stands before his mirror on the wall of his cabin, combing his curly, red beard, which tumbles down almost to his waist, and thinks how wonderful it looks.

Every Saturday morning, Redbeard gathers together all the fine things he has made, putting them carefully onto his cart along with any leftover wood the villagers might buy for firewood. Mabel, his beloved little donkey, faithfully pulls the heavy cart all the way to the market, where she receives her reward of a kind word, and a juicy carrot.

But Redbeard doesn't earn much money from the things he makes. Whilst he is content if he has enough money to buy hay for Mabel and food and warm clothing for himself, sometimes he struggles to achieve even this, and life can become very hard indeed.

One cold, dark, winter's evening, as the wind howled around his cabin, Redbeard had just lit a fire and was enjoying a bowl of hot soup, when there came a sharp knock on his door. When he opened it, he was surprised to see Lord Havalot of Havalot Manor standing there with his horse. Redbeard had never

expected such a grand, important person to call upon him.

"Good evening, sir," he greeted his Lordship. "Can I help you?"

"I hope so," said Lord Havalot.

"I've been out riding most of the day and seem to have lost my way. I need to return home to Havalot Manor. Is it possible you could point me in the right direction?"

Redbeard nodded. "Certainly." He gave Lord Havalot the directions he needed and warned him to take care, for snow was on its way and the weather would be stormy.

"Thank you, you are most kind. You're Redbeard aren't you, the carpenter? I have heard of your skill."

"Yes, sir. Thank you," replied Redbeard.

"Well, one good turn deserves another," Lord Havalot said. "As it happens, I need a new chair; a very special one. If you could make it for me, I would be most pleased and will reward you well."

"I would be honoured, sir," came Redbeard's honest reply.

Lord Havalot smiled, handed the carpenter two gold coins and described the kind of chair he wanted. Then he said, "I passed a grand tree not far from here. The tallest, most remarkable I've ever seen. Make my chair from the wood of that magnificent tree and there will be five more gold coins when you deliver it to Havalot Manor!"

Redbeard was delighted. He assured Lord Havalot that he would do his best work for him. Seven gold coins would buy him things beyond his wildest dreams! He would never have to skrimp and save again.

Redbeard and the Enchanted Tree

Lord Havalot mounted his horse, waved goodbye and cantered away home through the forest. Redbeard smiled broadly at his good fortune and dashed outside to share the good news with Mabel.

Early the next morning, Redbeard set about making the chair. He sorted through his stock of fine wood, but soon realised he did not have enough for what he needed. So, despite the harsh weather, he set out with his barrow, ladder and axe to the glade in the forest and the tree that Lord Havalot had described.

Redbeard knew the forest well and he had long admired this tree. It was the tallest and straightest tree in the forest. No other tree could compare with it. Its leaves, blossoms and berries were the colour of a rich, red sunset all the year round – even now in the harsh, dark months of winter. Redbeard knew it would indeed provide the finest timber needed for his Lordship's special chair.

Standing in front of it, however, Redbeard suddenly realised he did not wish to harm the tree. It had given him shelter and shade from sun and rain and kept him safe whilst sleeping under its lofty, blossomed branches at the time when he was building his log cabin. He felt the tree was almost a special friend. "But what can I do? Lord Havalot wants this for his chair. I can't disappoint him."

Redbeard stared at the beautiful tree, and shook his head. His conscience was troubling him greatly. But then he thought of the money he had already been paid by Lord Havalot. Also, of the five more gold coins that Lord Havalot had promised him.

"Times are so desperately hard, and I must earn a living," Redbeard said aloud as if trying to convince himself.

Still feeling guilty, he approached one of the tree's wide, low branches.

He hesitated for a moment and then climbed his ladder and struck the first blow with his axe. Redbeard thought he heard a groan. The tree seemed to shrink away from him and he almost fell, but amazingly one of the branches reached out and held him safely. Redbeard froze.

"Was that all my imagination? Did the tree really just groan and stop me falling?"

Redbeard and the Enchanted Tree

He wondered whether he ought to carry on. Redbeard told himself not to be silly. "It's only a tree after all – even though it is a very special one."

He tried once more, raising his axe and striking a blow. The same thing happened again. Alarmed, he was shaking now, but he knew he must carry on for he needed the wood. He struck the branch again and the tree groaned deeply once more. Redbeard felt the painful sound come up through the tree trunk from its roots. He tried to ignore his worries and, despite being full of concern for the beautiful tree, he struck the final blow and down came the large branch.

There was silence.

It had not been a happy task for Redbeard and he was glad when it was finally over and he was able to return home.

Daylight was fading fast. The cold darkness seemed to wrap around him as he trudged home through the snow. His kind heart was troubled; his chest ached. He needed rest from his thoughts, so decided not to work on the chair until morning. He needed restful sleep.

After saying goodnight to Mabel, he stood before his mirror and combed his marvellous red beard in the same way he did every night. It made him feel better and he had soon forgotten his worries over the special tree. He tumbled into bed and fell fast asleep.

Through the long hours of a restless slumber, Redbeard dreamed of silver shadows floating around the magnificent tree. Angry voices cried out, "It's your fault, Redbeard. It's all your fault!" again and again. The shadows, never quite taking human shape, tormented him as he slept. As the night dragged on, Redbeard's dreams became more troubled. He could see the tree was shedding its leaves and berries; its trunk was slowly shrivelling.

Redbeard and the Enchanted Tree

He sobbed in his sleep.

In the morning, Redbeard awoke bleary-eyed and exhausted. Looking around his room and realising it had all been a dream did nothing to ease his guilty conscience. He sat down to breakfast but he couldn't eat, so he decided to work on the chair. His troubled mind wanted it out of the way, so he worked hard on it all day, never stopping.

By nightfall it looked grand. It stood majestically in the corner of the room.

Redbeard ate his supper, pleased with his day's work. Then he stood in front of his mirror and combed his precious beard. Feeling content and with the previous night's dreams gone from his mind, Redbeard lowered himself onto the grand chair.

In a thousand years, Redbeard could never have been prepared for what happened next.

The chair sprang to life and tossed him out onto the floor! Redbeard was stunned. He tried again, thinking he must have somehow missed the chair or slipped off it. Again, he lowered himself onto the carved, wooden seat. This time the chair groaned – just like the tree had – and threw him right across the room. Redbeard shook his dizzy head, unable to believe what was happening. He tried once more, but again he was thrown from the chair.

Exhausted, bruised and fearful he fell asleep in the corner of his cabin. And the troublesome dreams returned.

The tree appeared once again but was now almost dead. There were no blossoms or leaves left on it; all the branches had died. Slowly, the tree was shrinking, disappearing. He could hear the voices again, louder than before, sobbing, crying out, "It's your fault, Redbeard! It's all your fault!" The silver shadows weaved about, forming shapes: pointing fingers, glowering faces, shaking fists. The angry voices continued taunting him whispering, "Look what you've done! Look what you've done!"

In his dream, Redbeard hid his face in his hands and wept. To his horror, he could feel his treasured red beard beginning to fall away, and by the time the sunlight sliced through his curtains to wake him, his beard covered the floor just like the dead leaves of the enchanted tree in his dream.

The carpenter awoke from his nightmares. He rubbed his eyes that were so swollen from weeping in his sleep. With a heavy heart, he splashed cold water on his face and looked up into the mirror. He stared at his beard. It was still there, full and red as always, but now he did not feel any joy or pride at seeing it. Redbeard stood quietly, thinking of his unhappy dreams that were still so very fresh in his mind. He sighed. He was most unhappy.

He tried to eat some breakfast, but it was no use. "I must go and see the tree," he thought.

The warm sunshine had melted what was left of the snow and, as he made his way through the forest, it felt eerie and quiet. He could hear nothing. No birdsong greeted him. Nothing. There were no little animals scurrying about. Even the wind was still. The forest seemed unfriendly and it frightened him. He hurried, anxious to see the tree.

"What will I find when I get there? Will my dream have come true? Oh, I hope not!" he mumbled in despair.

Then he saw it.

Redbeard and the Enchanted Tree

Aghast, he fell to his knees. His lovely tree was almost gone. The ground around him was covered with its dead leaves. He held his dizzy head shamefully in his hands. His heart ached and he sobbed.

"Look what you've done! This is entirely your fault," an angry voice cried out. "What are you going to do about it, Redbeard?"

Redbeard looked up. Standing in front of him was a crowd of little elves. Their silvery suits were the shadows of his dreams! Their leader asked him again, "What are you going to do about it?"

Redbeard stuttered as he replied, "I... I am so very sorry. Truly I am. I would do anything to put it right if I could."

Their leader smirked. "Anything? Then you must cut off your beard and bury it here, beneath the tree. Only by doing this will you put to right the great wrong you have done. This enchanted tree was our home and you have killed it. Now we are homeless. Do this before sunset or a curse will be put on all the wood you work on." Then the elves disappeared.

At first Redbeard was horrified at the thought of his nightmare coming true, but as he looked around him at the dying tree, he knew in his heart of hearts what he must do.

It was now late afternoon and Redbeard was back at his cabin. He was struggling with his conscience. He loved his beautiful beard.

With a spade over his shoulder and a pair of scissors in his hand, he hurried back to the tree, or at least to what was left of it. There he would place his lovely beard among the roots.

As he approached the tree, an eerie silence hung heavily all around him. He began to dig a hole. When it was ready, he picked up the scissors.

With tears flowing down his cheeks, he almost changed his mind. Then, with a smile, Redbeard realised that his beard would grow back. This was a small sacrifice to make to right his wrong. He began cutting slowly and carefully.

Soon, the magnificent, red beard lay in his hands. Bending down, he placed it in the hole, and then he carefully covered it and stared at the ground for a long while, waiting for something to happen. Nothing did.

Redbeard returned home and, as he reached his door, he turned to watch the setting sun and suddenly his whole being felt at ease. He knew he had just righted a terrible wrong.

That night, he slumbered in peaceful dreams. He saw the enchanted tree, but it had once again become the most beautiful tree in the forest. It stood majestically as the little elves danced around it, happily calling out to him, "We thank you, Redbeard. Sacrificing your beloved beard has saved our home."

Redbeard could see the tree in all its splendour and a smile remained upon his lips for the rest of the night.

At dawn, the winter's sun shone brightly through Redbeard's window, waking him. He jumped out of bed feeling happy of heart. He ate breakfast then looked into his mirror, his face still bare. He hoped his dream had shown him a truth. Then his eyes fell upon the chair in the corner.

He walked over to it. Carefully, he sat in it and waited. Nothing happened. He stood up then sat in it again and waited and waited.

The chair did not move. Excited, Redbeard was up and running as fast as his legs would carry him, right back to the glade to stand in front of the beautiful tree.

There it stood in splendour – more magnificent than ever before – just as he had seen in his dream! As his eyes filled with tears of joy, the elves appeared.

"Redbeard," their leader said, "you have proved you are an honest man. Our tree is restored. Go with our blessings. But never again cut the enchanted tree." Then they were gone.

Redbeard turned and walked slowly home, listening to the birdsong that filled the air and enjoying the gentle winter breeze upon his bare cheeks. The forest had lost its eerie atmosphere. As he reached the door of his cabin, he felt that a great burden had been lifted from him.

Later that day, he and Mabel carried the chair to Havalot Manor and Redbeard was paid his five gold coins and both Redbeard and Mabel lived a contented and very happy life together.

Redbeard and the Enchanted Tree

Redbeard was so grateful for his good fortune that he shared it with those less fortunate. He was a good friend of the people, and the forest. He became known simply as Red for his beloved beard, unlike the magnificent tree, never did grow back – a reminder from the elves that there are more precious things in the world than our own pride.

Somersaults

Twitch the squirrel sat perched on a low branch of his favourite tree, peering up at the garden fence. Waiting.

"Any minute now," he whispered. "Any minute."

Just then, two grey squirrels appeared on top of the fence, their bushy tails flickering. Twitch caught his breath as the pair scuttled along the narrow ledge, delicate and light on their toes.

"They're so elegant!" sighed Twitch, enviously. "So graceful!"

The first squirrel, Fliss, scuttled to one end of the fence while Scamp, the second squirrel, waited by the post at the opposite end. "Ready?" he called.

"Ready," said Fliss. "One... two... three!"

Boiiing! The fence juddered as the squirrels sprang into the air, stretching their legs wide. "Ooh," thought Twitch. "They look like furry shooting stars!"

Timing it perfectly, they landed and flipped onto their front paws, before somersaulting along the thin wooden fence.

It was a dazzling blur of fur and feet and before Twitch could blink, the squirrels were off again, leaping in a giant arc, so high they were almost flying. With a flick of their tails, they landed on the washing line that ran across the whole width of the garden. The line barely wobbled as they tiptoed to the end and dropped down, gripping the wire with their back paws. For a moment, they hung there like socks, until finally, they swung up and backflipped into a hedge.

Twitch could feel his heart pounding. "Oh, I wish I could do those things!" he said. "I wish I was like Fliss. I wish I was like Scamp."

He stayed hidden on his branch while the other squirrels darted from the hedge into another garden. Once they were out of sight, Twitch stumbled from the tree, digging his claws into the bark as he gingerly made his way down the thick trunk. He stood on the grass and scanned the area: no cats, no dogs, no humans and no squirrels. He needed to be alone – because no one must ever see this!

Twitch tilted his head and stared up at the fence. *Gulp!* "Here goes nothing!"

Taking a deep breath, he charged, scurrying, scrabbling and heaving himself up the fence. He clung to the top, peering into the next garden. It was all a bit fuzzy due to his wobbling head, but he could make out a small pond with cloudy, green water. *Yuck!* he thought. *I hate water!*

There was no time to look at ponds, though. Gripping the fence with his back feet, Twitch slowly let go with his front, until he was standing upright. Shaking, he pushed his arms out wide, trying to make a star shape.

"Ta daaaa!" He held his position for just a few seconds, legs wobbling with the strain. "I can do it!" he huffed, but his tummy suddenly lurched and he lost his balance. *Splat!* He tumbled to the ground in flurry of fur and leaves.

"Ouch!" Twitch lay completely still and waited for his head to stop spinning.

"Ha ha ha!" It was Scamp's voice.

Somersaults

"Are you trying to be a gymnast, like us?" asked Fliss.

Twitch peered through his tail and groaned as he saw the two squirrels on the washing line, swinging inside the peg bag. *Oh no! They must have seen the whole thing*, he thought.

"You looked like a falling frog!" said Scamp. "I've never known a squirrel with such bad balance. HA HA HA!" He wiped his eyes. "Accept it, Twitch. To be a gymnast you need inner balance and you haven't got any!"

The two friends sprang from the peg bag and over the hedge, laughing as they went.

Twitch covered his eyes, but his tears flowed regardless. After a while, he sat up, grabbed a leaf and blew his nose. "I'll just have to try harder," he said. "I may not have inner balance yet, but I'm going to find it!"

He waited until it was dark – when the stars twinkled and the moon glowed like silver.

Twitch was alone. Apart from one thing: determination.

At first, trying to get onto the fence was even harder than before – how could he balance on something, when he couldn't even see it? But after a while, Twitch began to trust his senses. He started to *feel* things using his whiskers, his tail and his claws. He started to *know* when a movement was right. The darkness became his friend and Twitch began using an inner balance that he didn't even know he had!

Night after night, he practised simply climbing the fence and standing up without falling off. Eventually, he could scamper all the way along the fence using only his back feet. Gradually, he improved: day after day, step after step. Every time he fell or slipped off the fence, he climbed straight back up it. "I won't give up!" he kept saying. "Never. Give. Up."

It was when he tried jumping that he struggled – always ending up on the grass, bumped and bruised. "I *will* do backflips!" he cried. "I *will* do somersaults. I *will* swing on the washing line!" But so far, these moves escaped him.

One day, Twitch was napping at the base of the fence when he heard a loud barking. He jerked awake and scrabbled up the tree trunk onto his low branch. "A dog? Please, no!"

"Oh, hello, Twitch!" It was Fliss lying on a higher branch. "Yes, it's a horrible hound! Listen to that dreadful barking!"

Next to Fliss, Scamp shuddered. "You'd better keep to the trees, Twitch. With your lack of agility, that monster will catch you no problem," he said.

"Yes," said Twitch, quivering. "I'll stay—"

"WOOFWOOFWOOF!"

The dog was so loud that Twitch lurched backwards. He tried to cling on, grabbing twigs, pulling leaves, but it was no use. *Bump, bash, clonk!* He bounced to the ground.

Scamp screeched at him, "Quick! Get up! The dog's coming!"

Scrambling to his feet, Twitch launched himself at the fence. *I can do this*, he thought. *I can!* The dog barked again, its angry growl rumbling closer, but Twitch didn't care. He was at the top of the fence! At last, it was his time to sparkle! He felt as if his bones were stretchy. Like he could twist and curve his body into hundreds of beautiful shapes. He powered along the narrow wood, somersaulting, backflipping and flicking his tail with pride. The world seemed to stop and there was nothing but Twitch and the bubbling joy inside him. He was floating! Flying! Oh, the wonder, the happi—

THUMP! Twitch jolted back to reality as the dog smashed into the fence, sending wobbles all the way through the wood. The fence swayed, slowly at first, and Twitch clung to his inner balance, his new-found strength. He dug his claws in, scratching at the planks, tearing out splinters, but he was helpless. The fence quivered like grass in the breeze.

And he fell.

Splosh! He was in next-door's pond!

Splashing and spluttering, Twitch staggered from the water and leaped up onto the fence. Desperate to shake off the smelly water, he vaulted over the other side, springing up high, star-jumping through the air and vaulting off the washing line before landing in the hedge.

"Twitch?" It was Scamp's voice. "That was awesome!"

"Where's… the… dog?" Twitch gasped, his chest heaving as he caught his breath.

"It's gone," said Fliss, coming to sit next to him. "Someone said 'rabbits' and it ran off. You were great! You backflipped and somersaulted and…" She paused. "I'm sorry we laughed at you. Everyone has to start from the beginning. Even we did!"

"It was wrong of us," agreed Scamp. "What you just did was simply marvellous."

"Really?" Twitch could feel warmth running from his nose to his tail.

"How did you learn those moves?" said Fliss. "Last time we saw you, you were… a bit shaky."

"I just kept trying," said Twitch. "And I never gave up."

"I hope you'll forgive us for laughing," said Scamp.

"Just imagine the displays we could put on with *three* talented squirrels!" said Fliss.

"I'm not sure," Twitch said, thoughtfully. "You really hurt my feelings."

"We understand," said Scamp. "But we truly are very sorry for being so mean."

Twitch considered the two squirrels: the two most hypnotising, beautiful gymnasts he'd ever seen and now they wanted to work with him! "However," Twitch began, "if you hadn't laughed at me, perhaps I wouldn't have tried so hard. Though, the dog helped quite a lot, too!" he said, laughing.

"Oh," said Scamp, looking confused. "So it was a good thing, then?"

"*No*, Scamp!" Twitch said. "It was still very mean of you. I'm just saying that you helped me in a funny sort of way."

"It's settled then?" Scamp grinned.

Fliss skipped with excitement. "So, will you join us?"

Twitch pretended to think about it. Then he grinned, too. "Yeah, if you'll have me."

"Fantastic!" The three squirrels high fived. "We'll be the Super Somersaulting Squirrels!"

"And our motto can be 'Never. Give. Up'!" said Twitch, his bushy tail twitching with happiness.

Supersonic Freddie Phonic

Freddie sat at the back of the class, leaning his elbows on the table. The teacher, Mr Blot, was marching up and down at the front, waving his arms about excitedly and pointing at words on the whiteboard.

I don't know why he's so excited, thought Freddie. *It's just a load of letters.*

All the other children seemed to understand the mysterious code. They all put their hands up, called out the answers, or charged to the front to write on the board. Whenever they did, Mr Blot would give them a round of applause and shout, "Good job!" or, "Well done, you're a super star!" Then he'd go over to the wide chart on the wall and slap a shiny star next to their name.

Freddie stared miserably at Jessica as she skipped across the classroom and covered the whiteboard with perfectly formed letters. Why did she find it so easy? Why did *everyone* find it

so easy? To Freddie, it was a blurred muddle –
Egyptian hieroglyphs made more sense to him.

"So these words all have *t* and *r* in them,"
said Mr Blot, pushing his glasses back on
his nose. "Who'd like to come and fill in the
missing sounds?"

There was a sudden draught as every single
person in the class thrust their hands up. But
Mr Blot was in a searching mood and Freddie's
heart sank. His teacher began walking up and
down, glancing at each pupil and saying, "Now,
it's always the same people volunteering. I
want someone else to have a go. Who hasn't
been up here for a while?"

Freddie could feel himself getting hot and
sweaty. Mr Blot was being kind. It wasn't
always the same people. It was everyone in the
whole class apart from Freddie. Freddie stared
desperately at the board. *What does it say*? he
thought.

"Freddie?" said Mr Blot, arriving at the
back of the room. "Would you like to come up
and have a go?"

"No, thank you." Freddie tried to dissolve
into the chair.

Mr Blot held out the whiteboard pen. "I'll help you. Let's give it a go, shall we?"

Freddie shook his head and wished he could disappear. But Mr Blot wasn't giving up today. "OK," he said, walking back to the front of the class. "You don't have to come up to the board, not if you don't want. But can you have a go at reading the word?"

Oh, please no! Freddie leaned forwards and squinted at the whiteboard. He could see lots of shapes, swirling circles and squiggly lines. Nope. He didn't get it. It didn't matter how many times Mr Blot said, "Sound it out" or, "Say what you see". Freddie had no idea.

Mr Blot was still smiling. "Give it a go."

Freddie's mouth was so dry, he could barely speak. "T…" he stammered. "T… h…"

"That's right, well done!" Mr Blot tapped one of the words with his pen. *"Then…* You read *then*! Super job. Super star! And here's a silver sticker for Freddie. Well done for trying."

Freddie sank back in his seat. He felt silly watching Mr Blot putting a sticker next to his name. He hadn't *really* got the word right,

had he? Mr Blot had basically done it for him. He glanced at Mason sitting next to him. Freddie could tell by the way Mason frowned, he knew Mr Blot was just being kind. It was embarrassing.

I just can't do it! Freddie stared up at the window, biting down on his lip. *I won't cry, I won't...*

He sat up, quickly. What was that? By the window there was a strange light. Glowing and shimmering.

Freddie tapped Mason's arm.

"What?" Mason frowned.

Freddie pointed. "Look!" he said, quietly. "Up by the window. It's a flashing light. All bright and sparkly."

Mason followed Freddie's outstretched hand. "Where?"

"There! Look!" Freddie bumped up and down in his chair.

"I can't see anything," said Mason. "You're making it up."

Freddie thought his eyes were going to pop out of his head because there was *definitely* something up there. The light was getting brighter and he could see a figure – arms and legs and a face! Oh! It was a person, a tiny person the size of a yogurt pot. Even more amazing, it was flying! It was hovering in the air outside the classroom!

Bursting with excitement, Freddie quickly scanned the room to see if any of his classmates had noticed but everyone was still writing, heads down, gazing at their work. As Freddie's heart raced, Mr Blot told them to clear away and go outside for break. "Come on, Freddie," said Mason. "I'll get the football."

"Yeah, I'll be out in a minute." Freddie watched as the class emptied and Mr Blot disappeared into his stock cupboard. By the time Freddie glanced back at the window, the small glowing creature had gone.

Freddie swallowed a lump of disappointment. He must have imagined it. But as he stood to leave, he gasped. The creature, the minute person, was sitting on his chair!

"Hello, Freddie," it said.

The creature flapped its tiny, transparent wings and floated above the desk. "My name's Pho."

Freddie stared wide-eyed as the creature fluttered to a small cupboard and landed on a pile of books. It was wearing green trousers and a shirt decorated with sparkly letters – the whole alphabet. As Freddie looked more closely, he could see the creature's hands and face were also painted with golden and silver letters. Each letter caught the light as the creature moved, creating the shimmering light that Freddie had first seen.

Pho ran his tiny fingers over some of the letters on the wall. "M-a-th-s," he said. "It spells maths! Oh, I love reading! Now let me see..." Pho sailed back to Freddie's table. "I'm here to help. You don't need to struggle

anymore. Not when I'm here!"

Freddie blinked. "You're going to help me?"

"Yes!" Pho floated above Freddie's workbook and placed his tiny foot on the writing. "*T* and *H* makes a what sound? *Th*–ink," he said, winking at Freddie.

"*Th*." Freddie grinned.

"YES!" Pho lifted higher into the air and sprayed Freddie with a handful of sparkles. "That's right. Now say it again. Watch my face... *th*."

Freddie giggled, enjoying the warmth from the shimmering glitter. There was just enough time to see that each sparkle was an individual letter of the alphabet, before they disappeared, melting into the table like snowflakes. He carried on giggling watching Pho's face. He had his eyes closed and his tongue sticking out between his teeth making the sound, "Thhhh."

At that moment, Mr Blot emerged from his cupboard, carrying a cup of coffee. "Freddie? Shouldn't you be outside? Go on, off you go. Get some fresh air."

Freddie jumped up, startled. "Er... yes... I'm just..." He waited to see if Mr Blot had noticed Pho, but the teacher slouched in his chair, slurped his coffee and opened a packet of biscuits.

"He hasn't seen you, it's OK," Freddie whispered, turning back to his desk. But there was no sign of his magical friend. Pho had disappeared. But amazingly, Freddie felt different. Something glowed inside him now, and it wasn't just sparkles. There was a feeling of hope. When Pho had pointed out 'th' to him, he'd understood it for the first time ever, and the two letters had blended together in Freddie's mind. He suddenly realised what Mr Blot and Mum and Dad had been trying to tell him for all these months.

I just needed Pho to explain it to me, he thought. *I just needed Pho.* And he ran outside feeling happy for once.

Next day, Freddie was worried that Pho had been a dream. How could a creature come through the window and help with your reading? It couldn't. As Mr Blot announced it was time for phonics, Freddie felt the familiar dread in his stomach. He sat back and waited for the lesson to be over. After a few minutes of Mr Blot pointing at letters and everyone else joining in, Freddie noticed a movement by the light fitting. His heart leaped as Pho floated from the ceiling like a spider descending on its line of silk. Freddie watched the miniature person hover above the children, sprinkling each head with colourful letters. When he reached Mr Blot, he sprayed the sounds straight in the teacher's face. No one else seemed to notice.

Finally, Pho landed on Freddie's shoulder. "Right, concentrate. What are we doing today?"

Freddie daren't speak out loud, so he just prodded his whiteboard where he'd been trying to write words that had the 'er' sound in them.

"Oh good," said Pho. "My favourite!" And he started to explain, landing delicately on each word, saying them slowly. Within a few minutes, Freddie felt something clear inside his head. It was as if someone had pressed the 'refresh' button. *I think I get it!* he said to himself. *I really do!* Excitement whizzed through his veins, filling him with new-found confidence. His head felt clearer. His brain was unblocked. He *wanted* to read!

The rest of the lesson raced by as Pho murmured in Freddie's ear, explaining the letters in more detail, dancing and cartwheeling over the whiteboard. He used simple words and short sentences. He explained things and it made sense! Freddie couldn't believe he was actually enjoying a phonics lesson.

And so it went on. Pho appeared every day. Even when Mr Blot moved the class to the library, just for a change, or out on the playground – Pho always found them. Freddie started to look forward to these lessons, excited at how quickly he was learning and thrilled by his own ability.

After the first week, Freddie had a sudden urge to raise his hand when Mr Blot asked a question. He didn't even hesitate, his arm just shot up.

Mr Blot looked shocked. "Freddie? Are you going to give it a go? That's marvellous."

Before he could change his mind, Pho nudged his shoulder. "You can do this. Get down the front and fill in that board!"

All eyes were on him, but Freddie didn't care. He took Mr Blot's pen and wrote the words on the board. "CORRECT!" Pho somersaulted in the air and gave Freddie a high five.

"YES!" said Mr Blot, clapping his hands. "Bravo, Supersonic Freddie Phonic! Spot on!"

Freddie grinned at the funny nickname his teacher gave him, and his classmates gave a little cheer.

"You did it!" Pho fluttered around, circling Freddie like a sparkling hoop, showering him with shiny letters. "Hooray for Freddie!"

Freddie soon had so many stars next to his name that Mr Blot had to widen the piece of paper.

Before long, Freddie started reading whole books, sharing them with Mum and Dad or enjoying them on his own. He received a Head Teacher's award for *Most Improved Reader* and all the children wanted to sit next to him because he could help them, too.

One day, Freddie realised Pho had missed a few lessons. It didn't matter too much

because Freddie found phonics so much easier now, but he did wonder where his brilliant friend had gone.

Later that same day, Freddie was in the playground when he noticed a faint yellow glow behind the PE shed. He rushed over to look and there was Pho, resting on a pile of leaves. "Hello," said Freddie. "What are you doing out here?"

"I'm going away for a while." Pho hovered over the leaves, scattering glittery letters everywhere.

"What?" Freddie swallowed. "How will I do phonics without you?"

Pho smiled. "I haven't been there for at least a week, but I've been watching. You can do it, Freddie, you always could. I just gave you a little help, that's all."

"But—"

"But nothing." Pho reached out and grabbed a selection of letters as they fell. "You've got it all inside your head, Freddie. You're a good learner and if you ever get stuck in your learning again, remember that." He spread the letters on the ground. "Remember, Freddie, you did this. You learned to read. Always believe in yourself." And he disappeared, leaving a spray of shimmering colours.

Freddie reached out to grab the letters but they vanished. He stared at the blank space where his friend had been. "Thank you, Pho," he whispered. "But I couldn't have done it without you."

He stared sadly at the ground and his tummy did a little jump as he saw the letters Pho had placed there. "Wow! These haven't melted!" He tried to pick them up, but they had merged into the concrete, pressed into the ground like tiny diamonds.

Maybe Pho was right. Maybe he would be OK on his own. After all, he had been managing without Pho for a while now. Freddie would try to be confident. He *was* a good learner and if ever he felt unsure of himself again, Freddie knew he could return to this spot by the shed and see the special message Pho had left.

"You can do it, Freddie!"

The Princess Swap

Princess Lola stared out of the window, watching a bird swoop past. It was a beautiful, warm, sunny day and she wished she could be outside, racing through the grass with the sun on her face – not stuck in this stuffy dining room in a huge, puffy, itchy dress.

Her parents, the king and queen, were busy chatting with the Duke and Duchess of Dingleby about something very boring that Lola didn't really understand. The problem with being a princess was that Lola never got to do the normal things that other children did. She couldn't remember ever having made a mud pie, climbing a tree or even just slouching in her chair. It was always, "Sit still, Lola", "Smile politely, Lola", "Don't run, Lola." That's all Lola ever did. Wear pretty dresses, smile politely, and keep quiet. It was very boring. It wasn't that she didn't love being a princess, she just wished she didn't have to be one *all* the time.

Downstairs in the kitchen, Martha was helping her mother put the finishing touches on the beautiful puddings about to be taken up to the dining room for the royal banquet. Martha loved helping her mother and seeing the amazing creations that the chefs made for the palace's lavish dinner parties. But just once, Martha wished that she could try some of the delicious food, and maybe sit at the fancy table in a beautiful dress, just like Princess Lola did. But she was just the maid's daughter, so Martha knew that it would never happen. She didn't own any dresses, let alone the beautiful ones the princess wore. Martha brushed some of the dirt from her jeans. It wasn't that she didn't love all the different and interesting jobs she got to do around the palace, but she just wished she didn't have to do them *all* the time.

Just then, Martha spotted a face peering around the side of the kitchen door. When it saw Martha looking, it quickly disappeared. Martha looked round the door just in time to see a flash of pink disappear into the bathroom. Martha wanted to know who it was that had been spying on them, so she followed. She was surprised to see the princess standing there, looking very embarrassed.

"I'm sorry," Lola said. "I wasn't spying. It's just that I never get to come down here and see what happens in the kitchen."

"But why would you *want* to be down here, Princess, when you can be up there, having fancy food at a beautiful dinner party?" Martha asked. "That's much more exciting than down here."

Lola laughed. There was nothing exciting about that dinner party, she thought.

"I would much rather be making the food. I'd love to cook, but Mother never lets me. It's not a princess's job, apparently," Lola said, rolling her eyes. "You're so lucky that you get to do whatever you like."

"I'm not as lucky as you," Martha replied. "I never get to wear beautiful dresses like yours. I wish I could go to one of your parties."

Martha stared at all the pretty jewels and lace on Lola's dress, wishing she could try it on, just for a moment.

The Princess Swap

Lola sighed. She looked at Martha in her messy, ripped jeans and cosy, soft jumper.

"I like your jumper," Lola said.

Martha looked down at the plain old jumper she'd had for years.

"I love your dress, it's so beautiful," Martha said.

"Thanks," said Lola, scratching her neck where the frills itched her. "Hey, do you want to try it on? And I could try on your jeans and jumper."

"Really?" gasped Martha.

The girls quickly swapped clothes. Lola thought Martha's clothes were so comfy, much better than those stiff dresses she always had to wear. Martha looked at herself in the mirror in the beautiful sparkling dress. She had never worn something so beautiful in all her life.

"Quick, we had better swap back before someone notices you've gone," Martha said.

Lola and Martha took one last look at themselves in the mirror.

"You look *just* like me in that dress!" Lola gasped.

Martha looked at herself. It was true, they

did look remarkably similar. They were both a similar height, with brown hair, and freckles on their noses. However, Martha's face was dirty and her curly hair hung in a mess, while Lola was neat and tidy with perfectly pinned curls.

"Why don't we swap places?" Lola said excitedly. "You could go to my dinner party and see what it's like being a princess for the rest of the day, and I could do all your jobs around the palace, getting messy and having fun."

"Are you serious?" Martha said in surprise. "Won't your parents notice?"

"No way, they are far too busy with the Duke and Duchess of Boring Town!" Lola giggled. "With you in this dress with your hair pinned up like mine they won't notice a thing. It's only for a few hours. What do you think?"

"OK, let's do it!" said Martha. She couldn't believe they were actually going to swap places!

Lola quickly fixed Martha's hair so that it matched hers, and told her all about what she should expect.

"All you have to do is sit there, smile politely, and don't talk," Lola said.

"That sounds easy. And all *you* have to do is follow my mum around and make sure nobody sees you," Martha said, ruffling up Lola's hair a bit.

They looked again in the mirror. It was simply astonishing just how alike they looked.

"We'll meet back here tonight after dinner and swap back, OK?" Lola said.

They both went their separate ways: Lola down to the kitchen, and Martha upstairs to the dining room.

When Martha opened the door, she stopped and stared. She had never been allowed in the dining room before. Even when her mum was cleaning she wouldn't let Martha in, in case she broke something.

"Well don't just stand there, Lola, come and sit down," the queen said.

Martha stared around the huge room. The ceilings were high and painted to look just like the sky with fluffy white clouds. A huge, golden fireplace stood at one end of the room with a warm, crackling fire in it, even though it was a warm day. The table was long, covered with a bright white tablecloth, and set with vases of beautiful flowers that Martha had helped to pick earlier that morning. It was the biggest, most beautiful room Martha had ever seen.

"Lola," the queen's voice came again, and Martha jumped. She was talking to *her*. Martha was supposed to be Lola! "Are you all right? You were gone a long time."

"Sorry," Martha mumbled quickly, keeping her head down and moving quickly to the empty place at the far end of the table.

Just then, the door opened and in came Martha's mother carrying a tray full of the beautiful desserts that Martha had been watching the chef prepare just moments earlier. Martha turned her head to face the window so her mother wouldn't get a good look at her. She was sure she was about to get caught. But then Martha heard the door close again and she looked up to see that her mother had already gone. She hungrily tucked in to the delicious pudding.

"Mmmm, this is yummy," Martha said. It really was the nicest thing she had ever tasted. When she looked up, Martha saw the king and queen staring at her from the other end of the table. To her horror, nobody else was eating.

"What's that, dear?" the queen said, looking slightly annoyed.

"Where are your manners? We always wait for our guests to start eating first, you know that," the king sternly reminded her.

"Oh, sorry," said Martha, her cheeks turning bright pink. "I was just... really hungry."

"Oh, don't worry about all that," the Duchess of Dingleby said kindly. "You're right, it does look delicious. Let's all start, shall we?"

Martha sat quietly, slowly eating the rest of

her pudding in silence. Lola had told her to sit quietly. If she wasn't careful, she wasn't going to make it through dinner, let alone to the end of the day. Martha only hoped that Lola was doing better than she was!

Downstairs, Lola was up to her elbows in soap suds. She had offered to do the washing-up while Martha's mother took the puddings upstairs. Lola had been sad to watch the delicious puddings go, knowing that this time she wasn't going to get any.

Lola blew a handful of bubbles and they floated across the kitchen. She grabbed another handful, and another, watching the tiny bubbles bob up and down before popping in mid air. Martha's mother came back in and Lola put her head down, pretending to focus really hard on the washing-up so she wouldn't look too closely at her

"Whoooaaaaa!"

Bang! Crash! SMASH!

Lola spun round to see Martha's mother flat on her back, and the tray and plates she had been carrying lying broken on the floor. Other staff came rushing to help her up.

The Princess Swap

"Did you make all this mess, Martha?"

Martha's mother looked at Lola expectantly. It took Lola a moment to remember that Martha's mum was talking to her.

"I didn't mean to, it was an accident. I'm sorry," Lola said, looking at the puddles of water she had splashed across the kitchen floor.

"You need to clean this up before anyone else gets hurt," said Martha's mum crossly as she began to pick up all the broken pieces of crockery.

Lola's cheeks burned with embarrassment as she helped to clean the floor, fighting back tears as she did. She wasn't very good at this swap. Not only had she made a complete mess, but she had hurt Martha's mum too.

Back upstairs, the real Martha stifled a yawn. It was hot and stuffy in the dining room, and Martha's beautiful dress was starting to get itchy and uncomfortable. Never mind, Martha thought, it was worth it to get to be a princess. But it wasn't going at all how Martha had imagined. They were still at the dining table after what felt like hours.

The king and queen were now having coffee, and cheese and biscuits, and were still deep in conversation with the duke and duchess about who knows what. Martha had enjoyed a cup of hot chocolate and a plate of biscuits, but she was now feeling sleepier and sleepier. She wondered if the king and queen ever did anything other than sit around the dining table, eating and talking. Martha was sure they would all still be sitting there when breakfast was served!

Martha gazed out of the window, wondering what Lola was up to, when she spotted her riding through the gardens on one of the horses. It looked like she was having a lot of fun, and Martha wished that she could be out there with her, messing around in the fresh air, not cooped up in this stuffy dining room. Perhaps being a princess wasn't as wonderful as she had thought it would be. It was certainly very lonely sitting here on her own.

Meanwhile, Lola was having a nightmare of a time. She had been asked to bring the horses in for the night, and at first she had had been so excited. She loved horses, but the closest

she ever got to them was when they pulled her carriage on royal visits. Lola wished she could take one out for a ride. She had never ridden before, but how hard could it be? All you had to do was sit there and the horse did the rest. So as she led a horse out of the gate, Lola decided to jump onto its back. She grabbed its back and pulled herself up, but instead of a gentle trot, the horse began to run! Lola hung on tight but it was no use and… *splat!* She fell off and landed in a muddy puddle as the horse cantered quickly away. Lola didn't know whether to laugh or cry. She had wanted to get muddy, but this was a little bit more than she had imagined! Her amusement quickly faded as she realised that she had left the paddock gate open... all the horses had escaped and were racing around the palace grounds! Lola ran after them, trying to round them up, but as soon as she got near them they scattered. They were having great fun, enjoying their freedom. Lola, however, was not.

Exhausted, and dirtier than she had ever been in her life, Lola rounded up the last horse just as the king and queen came out to take a stroll in the gardens with their guests. They looked right at her. Lola was sure they would recognise her, but they turned away as though they hadn't even seen her. How could they not realise who she was?

Lola felt miserable as she trudged inside. Her day was nothing like she had hoped it would be. She was so tired she could barely even stand, she was covered from head to toe in mud, and she stank of horse muck. Back in the bathroom, she looked at herself in the mirror. She barely recognised herself, no wonder her parents hadn't had a clue who she really was. Her hair was a mess and her face was covered in mud – she couldn't look less like a princess. It had only been a few hours, but she missed her mum and dad. Lola began to cry.

Suddenly, the door flew open and Martha burst in. Lola quickly wiped her eyes so that Martha wouldn't know she was upset. She was sure Martha was having the best day being a princess, and she didn't want to ruin it for her.

Martha stopped in her tracks. She had only come down to the bathroom to get a bit of fresh air, and she had hoped she might get to see her mum, too. But now Lola was here she would have to pretend to be having the time of her life. She didn't want Lola to think she was ungrateful.

"What happened to you?" Martha asked. "Don't tell me, the horses escaped again?"

"You mean they've done this before?" Lola asked, relieved that it wasn't all her fault.

"All the time!" Martha said, laughing. "I've lost count of the number of times I've had to chase those cheeky things back into the stables. I don't normally end up quite that messy though!"

Lola stared at her reflection in the mirror and both girls burst out laughing.

"So, how is your day being a princess? I bet it's going better than mine," Lola admitted.

"It's... fine," Martha said.

"You're bored stiff aren't you?" Lola said.

Martha was about to deny it, but she couldn't.

"I guess neither of us is having the day we were hoping for," Martha said. "Maybe it's time to swap back?"

"I suppose so," Lola said, secretly relieved.

Just then, the bathroom door opened and Martha's mother came in. When she saw the two girls together, she did a double take.

"Martha?" she said, looking from one girl to the other.

"Yes," said Martha, stepping forward.

"Well," said Martha's mum. "I think you two have some explaining to do, don't you?" The girls quickly told her about their day, how they had both wanted a change and had decided to swap places.

The Princess Swap

"I think we need to talk to your parents," Martha's mum said to Lola. "Let's get you cleaned up first."

Martha's mum helped Lola clean off all the mud, and then they went upstairs to find the king and queen.

"Lola, where have you been?" they asked Martha as the group walked into the royal living room.

"I'm Lola," Lola said, still dressed in Martha's dirty clothes.

"Lola?" the queen said, looking at her daughter, confused. "Why are you dressed like that? What's going on?"

Lola took a deep breath. She was worried she was going to get into trouble, but she needed to tell her parents the truth. If she didn't do it now then she never would. So Lola told them how boring she found the dinner parties, how much she wished she could play and get messy like other children, and how she had found a friend right here in the castle.

The king and queen looked at each other, and then at Lola and Martha. Lola held her breath, waiting for the shouting to start. But

Popular Rewards

it didn't.

"We're sorry," the queen said. "You are only children after all. Of course you want to play and have fun, and dress up. I can't see why you two can't play together."

"Martha, would you like to join us for dinner this evening?" asked the king.

Martha nodded happily, and then she hesitated. But I don't have a dress to wear."

"That's fine, wear whatever you are comfortable in. We all will. In fact, let's make it a pyjama party, and the whole palace is invited!"

Lola and Martha looked at each other in amazement. What a day they had both had!

That night, the whole palace came together for a pyjama party. They listened to music, played games, and even had a midnight feast. Everyone had a great time, and the king and queen realised they hadn't enjoyed themselves so much in a long time.

From that day on, Lola and Martha spent a lot of time together. Lola helped Martha with the horses and the cooking. Her parents even bought her a whole wardrobe full of jeans and comfy T-shirts that she could wear and get messy. And Martha often came to dinner with Lola, and was even allowed to come to some of their grand parties so that Lola would have a friend to keep her company – with the king and queen treating her to a special dress to wear on such occasions. The king and queen were much more relaxed. Life for everyone in the palace had never been so much fun.

"Thank goodness we told the truth that day!" Lola whispered to Martha one evening during a spectacularly boring banquet.

Martha wriggled in her dress and adjusted her lace collar for the hundredth time and said, "Do you think we can tell them the truth about these itchy dresses, too?" Both girls giggled – and scratched! – until the banquet was over!

The Wishing Pudding

Wizard Wipigast and Witchie Ephi have been the best of friends for quite some time now – although that hasn't always been the case. Before they were friends, they fought constantly. Who could cast the best spell? Who could ride the fastest (broomsticks and horses)? Who had the best cape? And so on – it was endless!

One particular day, they had a big fight out in the countryside where they had been racing their horses. Wipigast and Ephi had a noisy disagreement about who was the better rider, and Ephi had pushed Wipigast into the narrow river after he had magicked up a slow spell to spoil her horse's jump across it.

Watching the events unfold was an enchanted frog named Bozzwell. He was a mischief-maker and he saw an opportunity to have some fun. As Ephi rode off, leaving Wipigast soaked and fuming in the river,

Bozzwell hopped over to the wizard and offered to grant him three wishes. The wizard used one of them immediately. Tired of their constant bickering, he burbled, "I just wish Ephi and I were friends!"

Ephi, now suddenly overcome with worry and guilt, quickly turned her horse around and rode back to the river to pull Wipigast out of the water.

Both of them, standing on the bank, soaked to the skin, suddenly found it very funny. They laughed and laughed and each apologised for being so ghastly to the other. Wizard Wipigast invited Ephi home to his castle for tea and they have been the best of friends ever since.

Ephi was an excellent witch and, as the pair

grew up, Ephi magicked herself a castle next door to her best friend. She loved performing magic, and jets of coloured light and rainbow stars could often be seen shooting from her windows and chimneys as Ephi dreamed up another incredible new spell. Her castle was full of talking mirrors, moving portraits, self-cleaning crockery and a magnificent staircase with the most peculiar carpet that would transport you somewhere new each step you took!

Wizard Wipigast, on the other hand, loved cooking, and trying out all kinds of different recipes. Each year, the pair would hold a feast for all their friends to celebrate the day their feuding ended and they finally became friends.

This particular year, with many of their friends and family due to arrive for the feast, Wipigast decided to create something extra special.

That night, Wizard Wipigast presented his magnificent pudding.

"This," the wizard declared, "is a magic wishing pudding!"

There were gasps of delight from all the

children at the table.

"I made it myself," he told them proudly. Then he waved his wand and said, "Magic pudding, grant one wish once we have emptied our dish."

They all clapped and waited eagerly for their helpings to arrive.

With only one wish available, they all tucked in, taking a huge spoonful of pudding into their mouths and gulping it straight down, anxious to be the first to finish and make the wish.

A young wizard, barely six years old, was the first to finish and the others held their breath to hear what he would wish.

"We wish to meet the man in the moon! To say hello and fly back soon!"

Ephi, Wipigast and all their guests laughed with joy at the silly wish and immediately, dozens of brightly coloured broomsticks flew in at the door. There was a lot of laughter and cheering as they each took hold of one of the broomsticks and they all flew out together through the wide-open doors.

Up they soared, high into the night sky,

The Wishing Pudding

where the moon shone brightly and where there were even more surprises in store. Chairs and tables, cats and dogs all floated in the moonlit night.

Delighted by his visitors, the man in the moon chuckled with glee.

"What fun they are having!" And he followed too, wanting to join in the weird, wild, wonderful pudding party in the sky – for they had all brought with them their dishes, freshly filled to the brim with magic pudding, which they carried on eating as they sailed among the stars. It seemed that the more they ate, the more magical it all became.

However, all this racket woke the sun, and he was not at all amused – he had to be up early in the morning.

"If I don't get my beauty sleep, it will be a very cloudy day tomorrow, I promise you, and you won't like that, will you?" he warned.

But Wizard Wipigast just laughed. "Don't be such a spoilsport, Sun. Come and join us, and have some fun!"

The sun just grumbled some more before finally going back to sleep.

The Wishing Pudding

Very soon, everyone began feeling rather tired with all this energetic flying about, and decided it was time to go home. But no matter how hard they tried, no one could steer their mischievous broomsticks back down to Earth. They, too, were enjoying the freedom of being out and about and did not want to go back home at all.

"Oh dear, what are we going to do now?" Ephi was worried. She and her friend had been in many pickles over the years, but trapped in space on a broomstick was their stickiest situation yet!

Wipigast suddenly realised that he possibly had a solution.

"The magic frog in the river owes me two wishes," he said. "He will help us."

So the wizard called out, "Bozzwell, can you hear me? Can you help us, please?"

Suddenly, there was a *plop* and a shiny, green frog with a wide grin on his face, appeared on the wizard's shoulder.

"My, my," he croaked. "You're in a fine mess, aren't you, Wipigast? No doubt about it. You definitely are in a fine mess."

"Just help us, please, Bozzwell. You did offer me three wishes, remember, and I've only used one!"

The frog croaked.

Suddenly, wonderful colours filled the skies around them as the frog's magic took effect. Then the chaos all stopped. The skies were clear of broomsticks, flying furniture, cats, dogs and crockery, and Bozzwell the magic frog had disappeared.

Everything was back to normal. The friends and their guest found themselves sitting safely at the table in the big hall of Wipigast's castle, their pudding dishes quite empty in front of them. All was safely returned. Ephi and Wipigast sighed with great relief.

When everyone had gone home and they were alone, Ephi turned to her friend. "I think that we'd best not make any more magic puddings. Who knows what might happen next time? I thought we were going to fly round and round the moon for eternity!"

Wizard Wipigast nodded.

"Well, at least I have one wish left should anything go wrong again!" Wipigast chuckled.

The Wishing Pudding

"What did you wish for with your first?" asked Ephi. Wipigast froze. He had dreaded telling Ephi the truth – that their friendship was just a spell – but he really was an honest wizard and he bravely told her.

Ephi was silent. The wizard waited for her to explode with rage at being tricked. But instead she began to giggle.

"Actually, I have a truth to tell you…" And Ephi explained how she'd made a wishing pudding many years ago – the day Wizard Wipigast fell in the river, in fact.

The wizard laughed. "Do you mean to say that we both wished for the other to be our friend?"

"Exactly so," croaked Bozzwell, appearing in the corner of the room. "But neither of your wishes were granted."

"But how did we become friends then?" asked Ephi.

The frog laughed a long, hearty chuckle. "Don't you see? While many friendships feel magical, you can't actually magic up a friend! You were meant to be friends all along."

Wizard Wipigast and Witchie Ephi were

delighted. For years they had each felt such joy at being friends with the other, but such guilt at the wish they'd made to make it happen. To learn their friendship was real all along was the best news in the world – better than any magical wish they could imagine!

George and the Giant

George's family were very poor. That didn't worry him much, as somehow their mum usually managed to find a way to keep him and his brother Jack fed, even if she sometimes went without. But what did bother him was that all George ever heard was 'Jack this' and 'Jack that'. Even his mother often called him Jack by mistake. For some reason that George never quite figured out, Jack was the 'golden boy', and no one ever seemed to remember that he even had a younger brother! People always just knew their home as the farm where Jack lived. However, this particular story is all about George. But, like most of their stories, this one starts with Jack.

Jack had been sent to market to sell the family cow, Buttercup. George loved Buttercup. He was the one who had looked after her and cared for her. So, when Jack came back from the market and told them that he had traded Buttercup for just a few measly beans, George was appalled. Their mother was so cross with Jack that she threw the beans straight out of the window and sent him to bed without any dinner. George went to bed that night heartbroken for Buttercup, but glad that Jack was in trouble for once.

The feeling was short-lived though, as early next morning, George looked out of his window to see an enormous beanstalk had grown in the garden, stretching up into the clouds – and Jack was climbing down it, carrying a heavy sack on his back.

"Mum! Mum!" cried Jack. "You'll never believe what's happened!"

Their mother came sleepily out of her room and made her way downstairs. George followed. In a rush of words, Jack told them about the beanstalk and opened the sack to reveal more gold than any of them had ever seen in their lives. George's mother clapped her hand to her mouth in astonishment, then pulled Jack into her arms and hugged him.

"Oh, Jack, I knew you would never let me down! How clever of you to trade Buttercup

for those magic beans so that we could get all this gold. What a good boy you are! I should never have doubted you!"

George stared open-mouthed. He couldn't believe what was happening. How did everything *always* work out so well for Jack? There he was, all smug, like he knew this was going to happen all along. George was in a bad mood for the rest of the day.

"Where did you get that gold?" he asked Jack later when they were alone.

"It was just sitting at the top of the beanstalk." Jack shrugged. "It didn't seem to belong to anybody, so I just took it!" But George was sure he wasn't telling the whole truth. Over the next few days George kept a very close eye on his brother.

Then, two days after his first trip up the beanstalk, Jack crept out in the middle of the night and climbed up it again. George watched and waited until his brother returned, carrying something else. A golden harp!

"What have you been up to?" George asked as he ran out to meet him. "And what are you going to do with that harp?"

"Just you wait and see!" Jack laughed. "I'm going to show Mum."

He showed them how the harp magically played the most enchanting music all by itself. Their mother gasped in astonishment, then threw her arms around Jack.

"Oh, Jack. How clever of you to trade the cow for those beans!" And she sent Jack into town where people were so amazed by the harp, that they gave him lots of money to listen to the beautiful music it played.

George couldn't believe it. Once again, Jack had come out on top!

"I suppose the harp was just sitting at the top of the beanstalk as well, was it?" George muttered.

George and the Giant

"Yes," said Jack, not quite meeting his brother's eye.

But George was suspicious. Jack was acting very suspiciously. He was jumpy and kept looking up the beanstalk like he was expecting something to happen. Something didn't seem right, and George wanted to find out what was going on. So the next time that Jack went up the beanstalk, George followed.

When he finally crawled through the clouds, he couldn't believe what he saw – there was a whole land up there, and everything was *huge*. The grass towered above George and the trees were as tall as mountains!

Suddenly, George heard a deep rumbling sound and a loud moan, and then the ground began to quake. Without even a glance behind him, George sped back down the hole in the clouds, back down the beanstalk and sprinted into the house. A few moments later, Jack came bursting through the door, panting, this time clutching a chicken of all things.

"What's going on, Jack?" George demanded. "What was all that noise?"

"Oh, that? It's just an angry giant chasing

me," Jack said calmly, putting down the chicken.

"A *GIANT!*" Alarmed, George looked out at the beanstalk, half expecting to see the giant at their front door.

"Don't worry, he can't get down here. We're perfectly safe," Jack assured his brother.

"What's all this noise?" came their mother's voice, and both boys spun around to see her standing in the doorway. They both tried to look innocent. "You had better not be getting us into any trouble, George."

"*Me?*" cried George. It was too much. He stormed up to his room leaving his brother to explain. Not that Jack would, thought George, grumpily. Not when he's the 'golden boy'. And golden boy he was. For the chicken he had brought back down the beanstalk laid golden eggs! The family were now truly rich beyond their wildest dreams and their mother couldn't praise Jack enough.

"Oh, Jack, my golden boy! You wonderful son," she said over and over – clearly unaware of their colossal problem at the top of the beanstalk.

George and the Giant

George was livid. He barely said a word to anyone for the rest of the day – not that they had noticed. Jack had taken the chicken into town and sold the eggs for even more gold.

That night George was so cross he couldn't sleep, so he went for a walk outside. He'd not gone far when he heard a strange noise. It sounded like someone was crying, and it seemed to be coming from the top of the beanstalk. Someone was up there. What if they were stuck and needed help escaping from the giant?

Carefully, George climbed up the beanstalk. When he could finally see above the clouds, he nearly slipped right back down. A giant was sitting in the grass, head in his hands, shoulders shaking, and sobbing uncontrollably. George was about to flee, but something made him stop. The giant was clearly upset about something. So George nervously cleared his throat and said, "Excuse me. Are you all right?"

The giant looked up in surprise.

"Is something wrong?" George asked again.

The giant just blinked at him as his bottom

lip began to wobble. George began to think that perhaps the giant didn't understand him, or maybe he couldn't speak. But then the giant wiped his tears away and said, "You aren't the boy who's been coming up here."

"No," said George. "That was my brother, Jack. I'm sorry he's been stealing things from you. I'll make sure he doesn't bother you again."

The giant sniffed and George passed him his hanky. It was tiny in the giant's huge, bucket hands, and when he blew his nose the force blew George backwards.

He handed the hanky back, but George told him to keep it.

"Thank you. I'm Titch," said the giant, holding out his hand.

"I'm George." George attempted to shake the giant's hand but, in truth, it was so large that the pair did a sort of up-down high five instead.

"Nice to meet you. No one ever visits me up here. I get so lonely."

"Is that why you're crying?" George asked.

"Not really," said the giant. "You see, your brother took my harp, and now I can't sleep. I hate being all the way up here, I'm afraid of heights, and that harp was the only thing that calmed me down. When your brother started coming up, I hoped he might be able to help me get down from here, but he always ran away so quickly I couldn't catch up to ask for his help. And now, without my harp, I've been lying awake, terrified of falling. So I decided to sit here and wait for him to come back, so I could ask for his help."

"Can't you just climb down?" George asked.

"Have you *seen* how far down it is?" Titch shuddered at the thought. "Besides, even if I did make it down, what would be the point? I would still be alone. Nobody ever wants to be friends with me."

George looked at the giant. He was extraordinarily big, but he actually seemed very gentle and friendly.

"I'll be your friend," George said.

The giant blinked his huge eyes at George in amazement. "Really?" He grinned and picked George up in one giant hand and gave him a big hug – a little too tightly for comfort.

"And I will help you get down from here, too," gasped George as Titch let go. The giant looked like he might be about to give George another bone-squashing hug, so George ducked out of the way. With a promise to come back first thing in the morning with a plan to help Titch, George carefully climbed back down the beanstalk and slipped sleepily back into bed. He fell asleep wondering how on earth he was ever going to get a person the size of a house down a spindly beanstalk – and if he did, how would people react?

George and the Giant

By the time the sun had finally risen, George had made a plan. But he was going to need some help. He went to his brother's room and shook him awake.

"Jack! Come on, we need to go back up the beanstalk."

"Not today, we've got enough gold for now," said Jack, rolling back over and pulling the pillow over his head. But George pulled it straight off again.

"Not everything is about gold, Jack. Now come on," George insisted. Jack looked at George like he had lost his mind.

"Please?" George added hopefully.

"Fine!" snapped Jack, throwing back the bedclothes.

As the two of them got close to the top of the beanstalk, George heard Titch sniffing. He was still there, waiting for them.

When Jack saw the giant, he immediately tried to climb back down the beanstalk again, but George grabbed hold of him and pulled him up.

"What are you doing?" Jack whispered. "Don't you know what that is?"

"Yes," said George. "And that's why we've come. He needs our help, Jack. He's actually really nice – just lonely, and really scared of heights. We have to find a way to help him get down."

"Are you serious?" Jack was appalled. "That's a *giant*! Don't you know they *eat people*?"

"His name's Titch. And I'm pretty sure he doesn't eat people. Just give him a chance," said George.

Jack still wasn't sure, but his brother looked like he really wanted his help. So, reluctantly, he agreed.

They pulled themselves up to the top and George walked over to the giant.

"You came back?" said Titch, surprised.

"Of course," said George. "And I brought help. We're going to get you down onto the ground."

George looked back at Jack who was still hovering by the hole in the clouds, ready to make his escape.

Titch lunged at George, and Jack let out a yelp. But then he realised that the giant wasn't attacking George. He was hugging him!

"Right, let's get you down. I've got a plan," said George when the giant had finally put him down. "You're going to close your eyes tight and I'm going to sit on your shoulder and talk you through it, and Jack will help guide you slowly down the beanstalk. Are you ready?"

Neither Titch nor Jack looked like they thought the plan was going to work, but it was the only one they had. The giant was so desperate to get down from the land in the clouds, and he trusted George, so he nodded.

George climbed up onto Titch's shoulder, close to his ear, and the giant sat down carefully at the hole in the clouds. Jack climbed down the beanstalk just ahead of the giant. He was tempted to keep going down alone and to leave the giant stuck at the top, but he couldn't abandon George, so he grabbed Titch's huge ankle and told him he was ready.

"I can't do it," said Titch, peering down at the long drop to the ground. He started to tremble.

"Don't worry, just keep your eyes closed

and imagine you're walking on solid ground. You'll be fine," George whispered in his ear. He wrapped his arms around the giant's huge neck and gave him a comforting hug. Titch felt a little better. Then he closed his eyes tightly and lowered himself backwards down the hole onto the first branch of the beanstalk, with Jack guiding his feet. They went slowly, one branch at a time, until finally they had made it safely to the bottom.

Once they were down, Jack ran indoors to fetch their mum. When she saw the giant she froze, horrified.

"George, what have you done?" she gasped.

"Don't worry, Mum," said George, as Titch helped him down from his shoulder. "He's very friendly. He just needs somewhere to stay. I thought maybe he could live with us? Maybe in the barn?" Their house was clearly not large enough.

George's mum was still in so much shock that she couldn't say a word. Titch didn't say anything either. He was afraid that George's mother was going to send him back up the beanstalk.

George and the Giant

"Please, Mum," begged George. "He could help us. He's big and strong, he could work on the farm. I promise he won't be any trouble. I've never asked you for anything before."

Behind him the giant nodded, wide-eyed and hopeful. George's mum looked from George's pleading face to the giant's scared one, and back again.

When their mum learned that Jack had been stealing from the giant, she made Jack apologise for his thieving, and agreed that Titch could stay with them. George gave his mum the biggest hug. Then Titch scooped them both up into a gentle embrace.

Titch settled into life on the farm very quickly. He was so strong that he easily worked harder and faster than George, Jack and their mother put together. They used some of the golden eggs to pay for an enormous barn to be built for Titch to live in, and he was very happy there. Jack apologised for stealing from him and running away, and Titch graciously forgave him – though Jack still kept his distance a little bit. And of course, Jack was no longer the centre of attention.

George and the Giant

Their farm was no longer known as 'the farm where Jack lives', but to people far and wide it became known as 'Beanstalk Barn'. It took their mother some time to get used to having Titch around. But eventually she chatted away to him while they went about their daily work, like he was an old friend and soon enough she couldn't remember what life had been like before he had arrived. And as for George, Titch had never imagined he would find such a loyal friend, and George felt exactly the same way.

No Slugs for Sadie

It was very early morning and the birds were hardly awake. Frost dusted the grass, and if you looked carefully, you could see a young hedgehog scurrying across the crisp lawn. This was Sadie and she was on her way home. Through the long grass, she followed the pathway made by her own little paws and trotted past the shed at the end of the garden. Finally, she recognised her own Home Hedge and hurried inside the thick bushes.

Aunt Eve was waiting by the front gap, holding a clump of worms in her mouth. "Where have you been?" She dropped the worms on the ground. "These won't keep forever, you know. They're already starting to dry out."

Sadie nestled into her special dry-leaf pile and stared at the pink strings. "I'm not very hungry," she said. "I ate a slug just now, a... er, a huge fat one."

Aunt Eve's prickles lifted up and down like a wave. "Now come on, Sadie," she said. "We both know you hate slugs. You told me they were much too chewy."

Sadie clawed a small hole in the leaves. "Erm… I've changed my mind. That last slug was yummy."

Sadie sniffed one of the dried worms while her aunt shuffled into the back of the hedge to sleep for the day.

"I hate worms," whispered Sadie, pushing them under a stack of twigs. "They're chewy and gristly and taste of mould. And I hate slugs too – they're yucky, slimy, chewy – I'd rather eat pondweed than a slug." As she spoke, a light breeze lifted a branch from the hedge and the weak sunshine sparkled into her eyes. "Pondweed. Of course! I'll try eating pondweed!"

The following evening, the moon was high in the sky by the time Aunt Eve set off for more slime hunting. "I won't be long, Sadie," she said. "Stay in Home Hedge and don't—"

"Yes, Aunt Eve," Sadie yawned. "Don't talk to cats, dogs or humans."

Aunt Eve nodded and checked left and right, before scuttling into the garden, keeping close to the hedge.

Once her aunt had disappeared from view, Sadie stepped out of Home Hedge. Her prickles tingled with excitement as she caught sight of the pond glistening by the fence at the far side of the garden. "Delicious pond food, here we come!"

Sadie and her aunt visited the pond every day to drink the cool water, but she'd never tried the green fuzz floating on the surface. And she'd never tasted the tall leaves that grew in thick clumps at the edge of the water. They towered over the hedgehogs and Sadie thought they looked fresh, juicy and delicious – so much yummier than slugs or snails or worms!

Arriving at the pond, she crawled down the muddy bank and dipped a tiny toe in the water. A clump of pondweed drifted towards her and she lowered her face to drink. SLURP! It was OK, a bit watery, a bit bland. Sadie brushed off her disappointment and stepped further into the pond. Aha! Now she could see some reeds that looked tall, magnificent and surely delicious! She leaned up on her back legs and sank her teeth into the green flesh.

"Ergh!" she spat. "Ergh!" She tried to spit it out, but the leaf was glued to the roof of her mouth and, worst of all – worse than anything – it tasted horrible! Like ancient worms left in the sun. Like snail slime mixed with rabbit droppings. Sadie plunged her face in the water and slurped at the pond before staggering back up the slope and flopping against a soft, grassy mound.

"Bother," she said, spitting out the last of the reed. "That's even *more* disgusting than slugs!"

She leaned into the mound and tried to get her breath back, but something felt odd, strange, like the whole world was moving up and down!

"Whoa!" Sadie cried as the mound kept on moving – lifting and rippling in a most alarming way. She scrambled clear, watching the mound in amazement as it grew a pair of pointed ears, jagged white teeth and two sparkling eyes. Sadie gasped and rolled into a tight ball.

This wasn't a grassy mound. It was a cat.

"Those spines of yours are shockingly sharp. Woke me up, you did. I was having a lovely dream, all about mice," said the cat.

Sadie rolled out of her ball and hid behind a watering can.

"No need to hide," said the cat, stretching. "I won't hurt you." As if to prove it, the cat toppled onto his back and started washing his tail.

Sadie had seen cats before, but never this close. She'd always been in the safety of her hedge, with Aunt Eve forming a barrier between her and the terrifying creature. But now the huge monster was right in front of her! Sadie could see its thorn-like teeth and its giant, wide feet – big enough to squash a little hedgehog! She suddenly wished she'd stayed in her hedge.

The cat finished washing its tail. "Are you still there?" he said. "Can you come out from behind that watering can?"

"No," said Sadie, backing away. "I'm not allowed to talk to you."

The cat lifted an ear. "Not *allowed*?"

Sadie shivered. "Yes. Because you're dangerous."

"Dangerous? How on earth can I be dangerous?"

"Well…" Sadie stared at the cat as he lay stretched out on his side. She had to admit, he didn't look very dangerous. "You kill mice," she said. "And…"

The cat sighed as if it was a huge effort. "Oh, I *used* to. Many moons ago, when I was a fresh scamp. But I haven't got the energy now. Really can't be bothered, and anyway" – he glanced back at Sadie – "I've never eaten a hedgehog! Pah!" He pretended to spit on the

ground. "All those prickles! It would be like munching a clump of brambles!"

Sadie didn't mean to, but she found herself giggling. She tried to stop smiling. "Yes, but you could be just saying that to trick me. My aunt says I must stay away from you, so... erm... bye."

"But wait. Don't go!" The cat heaved himself upright. "No one ever talks to me anymore." His long, white whiskers drooped. "Everyone thinks I'm old and useless. Even my owners find me dull."

Sadie wanted to go home, but this cat looked so sad. "I'm sure you're not dull."

"Thank you! Oh, you're so kind!" He edged closer and gently nudged Sadie with the top of his head. Sadie closed her eyes. *Help!* she thought. *I'm going to be eaten by a cat! Aunt Eve will find my body in the morning – just a pile of prickles and nothing else.* She opened her eyes.

"Are you really not going to eat me?" said Sadie.

"Of course not!" He pointed to his round stomach. "I'm not even hungry. My owners give me so much food. And even if I was starving, I wouldn't eat you – not with all those spikes."

Sadie smiled. "But I should still be going home."

"What's your name?" the cat said. "I'm Arthur."

Sadie twitched her nose. "I'm Sadie and I'm not supposed to be out. If my aunt—"

"Don't worry, Sadie," said Arthur. "I'll make sure you get back in one piece, I promise," he purred. Sadie shuddered slightly when he said, 'in one piece'. What if he was lying? What if he was planning a hedgehog kebab right now? What if— her thoughts were interrupted as Arthur went on. "Now tell me why you were leaning on a poor old podgy pud like me."

Sadie felt herself blushing under her spines. "I didn't know I was leaning on a cat. I thought you were a hill."

"Ha!" Arthur threw his head back. "I've grown so large I now resemble a part of the landscape!"

"I'm sorry," said Sadie. "I hope I didn't hurt you. I just needed to rest on something."

Arthur swished his tail. "You didn't hurt old Arthur. I'm as tough as tyres. But what shocked you?"

Sadie glanced at the pond as it glimmered in the moonlight. "I was eating reeds and they tasted horrible."

Arthur's eyes grew wide. "Why would you eat reeds? Aren't you supposed to eat slugs and snails? They're the things that make you grow big and plump... er, *strong*."

Before Sadie could answer, an ear-splitting

bark shook the garden and Arthur seemed to jump right out of his skin. "DOG!" he yowled, his fur standing up on end. "RUN FOR YOUR LIFE!" He scrambled to his feet and pounced at the wooden fence, desperately trying to climb it.

Sadie watched in horror as Arthur's claws scraped and slipped on the wood, his tail spiked to twice its original size. As he continued to climb and slip, climb and slip, a square of golden light hit the garden. The back door of the human house opened and a large dog zoomed towards them.

"Run!" shouted Arthur. "Save yourself! It's a dog, a nasty, vicious dog!" Sadie was just in time to see jagged teeth, a lolling tongue and wild, staring eyes before she scuttled down the slope, into the thick reed bed.

"Woofwoofwoof!" The dog reached the fence and snapped at Arthur's dangling tail. By now, the poor cat was clinging on by his two front paws and Sadie's spikes quivered with fear. *Don't hurt him*, she thought. She trembled among the reeds and suddenly spotted a stone at the edge of the water. It gave her an idea!

No Slugs for Sadie

Creeping out from her hiding place, Sadie pushed the stone with her foot. Nothing. It wouldn't budge.

"Woofwoofwoof!" went the dog.

Sadie pushed again, and still the stone refused to move. Panic made her strong, and she leaned forwards and pressed the top of her head against the stone. At last it began to roll and she put all her weight behind it, heaving, pushing, gasping, until...

SPLOSH!

The stone hit the water, Arthur slipped off the fence and the dog stopped barking. Quickly, it turned its head and looked to see where the noise had come from.

"Uh oh," said Sadie quietly. "Maybe I shouldn't have done that!"

The dog thundered towards the pond. Now its wet nose was just in front of her. She could feel its hot breath, hear its dribbling tongue and smell its doggy fur. She closed her eyes. *I'm sorry, Aunt Eve. I didn't mean to disobey you.* And she folded in on herself, curling into a ball once more. She felt the dog push at her with its nose.

Suddenly, Sadie knew nothing apart from her own beating heart.

She had no idea how long she stayed scrunched up like that, but her legs were beginning to ache when she heard a voice.

"The coast's clear. You're safe to come out now, hedgehog."

It was the dog! She could feel its stinky breath on her as he spoke. No way was she coming out – it was a trick!

"Well done, Rusty. That pesky cat has gone now." Another voice. A human. "I'm not having it terrorise our garden anymore! Upsetting the wildlife and... well, oh, just ghastly!"

Sadie peeked out from her ball of spikes to see the human, with gloves on her hands, bending down to look at her.

"You had a lucky escape," said the dog to Sadie. "That cat's a real charmer you know. I bet he told you he doesn't eat mice anymore. It's all a trick. Acts all nice and friendly then..." Rusty didn't finish his sentence – just like the human. Sadie shuddered. He didn't need to. She knew what he meant.

No Slugs for Sadie

"Oh dear," she said, uncurling from her protective ball. "I've been so silly. Aunt Eve told me to stay at home, not to talk to strangers and I didn't listen and I was almost…" Sadie didn't finish her sentence either.

"Hello, little one," said the human, stretching out her gloved hands to lift Sadie. But before she could, a rustle erupted from the bushes and Sadie heard a familiar snorting bark.

"You get your hands off my niece," barked Aunt Eve. Of course the human couldn't understand a word she said, but she understood what she meant.

"Oh, my! Look at that, Rusty, an adult hedgehog. It must be coming to defend the little one," she said to the dog. The dog, no longer the fierce beast, lay down on the grass and wasn't one bit bothered by the charging hedgehog. The human stepped away and Aunt Eve gave Sadie the telling-off of her life.

"Oh! Look, it's happy to have found the little one," cooed the human, completely misunderstanding the interaction in front of her.

"I told you to stay at home! I told you not to talk to strangers!" barked Aunt Eve as she marched Sadie back to Home Hedge. "That horrible cat could have..." But she didn't finish her sentence.

"I'm really sorry, Aunt Eve," said Sadie. And she really was. "Because I lied to you. I left Home Hedge because I wanted to try some pondweed. I thought I could eat that instead of slugs and worms. I really don't like them. I didn't eat a slug yesterday. And I didn't eat the worms you gave me either."

Aunt Eve could see how upset her niece was. And how frightened she'd been by the events of the evening. "It's important that we tell the truth. I do wish you had been honest with me about not liking slugs and worms. We could have found something else for you," said Aunt Eve. "And I know you think I'm a doddery old fuddy-duddy, but can you see now why I told you to stay at home and not talk to strangers?"

"Yes, Aunt Eve. I'm really sorry. I'll be honest with you from now on, I promise."

"You're lucky. Not all strangers are friendly and helpful like that human and her dog. That cat could have…" Suddenly, there was a snuffle at the hedge and a giant paw loomed into view. The two hedgehogs huddled together, terrified.

"Don't panic, it's only me, Rusty." The dog shuffled onto his belly and poked his nose into the hedge so the hedgehogs could see him. "I've got a surprise for you. Follow me." Aunt Eve looked unsure, but Sadie smiled, following the dog back out from under the hedge. Aunt Eve scuttled after them.

Rusty led the two hedgehogs up the garden, just a little way from Home Hedge.

"What's that smell?" asked Sadie, her eyes lighting up and her mouth watering.

"It's for you. Both of you," said Rusty and he nudged a plate of delicious-smelling meat towards Sadie and Aunt Eve. "There'll be one every night, if you want it. And I'll be around to make sure that sneaky cat, Arthur, doesn't bother you again." And with that, he trotted back to the house.

"Thank you!" Sadie called after him. She could see the human standing by the door, smiling at her. The food was a gift from her,

Sadie understood.

Starving and unable to resist the smell any longer, Sadie spun around to try the food the human had put out for them and she couldn't believe what she saw.

"It's delicious!" said Aunt Eve, her mouth stuffed full of the tasty meat.

"Better than slugs and snails and worms?" laughed Sadie.

"Absolutely!" Aunt Eve said.

"Really?"

"Honestly!" winked Aunt Eve. "No more slugs for Sadie!"

Hector's Hens

Hector the horse sighed heavily and peered over the top of his stable door. "Where's Mr Cartwright got to with my supper?" he said to himself. "I've been on my own all day."

The sun was dipping below the trees and Hector's breath made puffs of steam in the cold evening air. He hated evenings – the way the sky seemed to come down all around him and the scary shadows creeping through his paddock. "I wish I had a friend," he said, resting his long nose on the lower part of his door. "Someone to tell me stories and keep me company."

He gazed into the distance where he could see a flock of chickens gathering together in a far-off field. Hector liked watching them. Sometimes he could hear their cheerful clucking and their comforting coos. No one would ever feel lonely or afraid with those feathery friends around.

A twig suddenly snapped in the nearby hedge and Hector jerked his head to look. "Oh blast and bother," he groaned as he caught sight of a shiny black nose and two pointed ears. It was Finlay Fox.

"Evening, Hoofy," said Finlay, tiptoeing out of the hedge.

Hector gave the fox a hard stare. "Don't call me Hoofy."

"All right, keep your mane on!" Finlay glided past a clump of nettles, his bushy tail dancing. "What's got you in such a grump?"

"I'm not in a grump," said Hector. "I just don't like the way you scare the chickens and chase the rabbits. It's not very nice!"

Finlay's yellow eyes glowed. "It's not me

who scares them – it's you! They can't wait to escape from your long, miserable face," he said meanly.

"How dare you?" said Hector, flicking his ears back. "Animals love me."

"No, they don't," Finlay crept forwards and leered up at Hector. "They think you're boring and smelly and that you're a mangy old mule."

"*What* did you say?"

"I said," Finlay scraped his claws down Hector's door, "you're a mangy old mule."

Crash! Hector headbutted the door, shattering its hinges. Finlay yelped, jumped in the air and landed on his back. Eyes wild and shocked, he scrambled to his feet and hurtled out of the paddock, slipping on the wet soil.

"Come back here!" shouted Hector, galloping after the fox. "I'll get you! I'll trample your fluffy tail, I'll jump on your—"

But Finlay was too fast. "You can't catch me, Hoofy!" he snarled. "You'll never catch me!" And he disappeared into the darkness.

Hector kept galloping, thundering over the grass, the wind whipping through his mane. Now that he was running, he couldn't stop.

It felt so good to be out of that stable, to feel the earth beneath his hooves, smell the sweet grass. Faster and faster he charged, pounding the field, until all of a sudden he saw a fence right in front of him. "HELP!" he whinnied, trying to slow down, but it was too late. He smashed through the fence, skidding and gouging four hoof-shaped trenches in the ground.

Squawk!

Hector caught his breath and looked up to see a flurry of brown feathers spiralling wildly.

"Oh my goodness and bless my hooves," he said. "I do believe I've crashed into the hen house!"

The hens scattered in all directions, flapping their wings and squawking in terror.

"I'm so terribly sorry," said Hector, breathing fast. "I really didn't mean to scare you all. My brakes aren't so good you see – the old trotters don't get much practice these days." He turned away, head down, tail drooping. "I'll be on my way, ladies." And he began to plod home again. After a few steps, he felt something pecking his left front hoof. He stopped walking and glanced at the ground, where he saw a small chicken.

"Sorry, I'm sorry," he said, assuming she had come to tell him off for causing such a mess.

The chicken was pulling at something on hector's hoof. "Stand still a minute," she said. "You've got a worm in your foot. Can I eat it?"

"Oh, yes… by all means. Help yourself." Hector nodded in bemusement.

The hen gripped Hector's hoof with her claws and pulled out a wriggling worm.

"Delicious," she said. "So fresh and juicy! And you did all the hard work, digging it up for me."

"Well, I didn't mean to—"

"Ooh, look, there's more!" The hen flapped her wings. "GIRLS! OVER HERE! FOOOOD!"

Hector had no time to move. A crowd of shrieking, clucking hens zoomed towards him. He tried to back away, but the birds covered him like a feathery blanket. At first he was alarmed, but soon he realised they were being quite gentle. It was his hooves they wanted – the large muddy clumps that carried so many worms.

"Gosh, that tickles!" said Hector, as four more hens jumped on his tail and back, waiting for their turn. He laughed and began to wobble across the field, swaying and lurching from side to side.

"This is fun!" cried one hen, clinging to Hector's mane. "It's like riding on Mr Cartwright's tractor, only less noisy! Weeee!"

Soon, more hens were queuing up to ride on Hector. He galloped around, swishing his tail, flicking his mane and pretending to wobble and throw the chickens off.

At last, Hector stopped for a rest and the chickens flapped to the ground.

Hector snorted through his nose. "Well, that was a lot of fun, girls! It's ever so lonely in that paddock. You know, I often—" he stopped and his ears pricked up as something rustled in the hedge. A snapping stick. A trampled leaf.

Hector peered closely. "Oh, my golly gosh, no!" His heart sank at the sight of two yellow eyes, glowing like poisonous caterpillars. "It's the fox!" he boomed. "Watch out everyone! It's Finlay Fox!"

Feathers flew as the hens launched themselves at Hector, flapping and scrabbling at his tail, his legs and his back. "Save us!" they screeched. "Please, Hector, we need you!"

Hector felt himself disappearing beneath a cloud of chickens. "It's OK," he whispered. "Keep calm, I'll look after you!" He glanced under a hen wing, just in time to see Finlay sneaking into the field, oozing out of the undergrowth like an oil stain.

"What's this?" Finlay caught sight of the strange hen-covered creature towering

above him. "It's got four legs and hundreds of glinting eyes!" Finlay started to shake, backing away. "And... oh! Look at all those sharp beaks!"

Underneath the chickens, Hector laughed. "He thinks I'm a monster! Finlay's scared of me!" And he began to whinny a rumbling giggle. Muffled by all the feathers, Finlay didn't recognise the sound.

Finlay's whiskers wobbled and his mouth fell open. "It makes the most terrible sound!" he gasped. "Like a howling beast... like a murderous monster... like nothing I've ever heard before!"

Hector laughed again and Finlay crumpled, his body squashing in on itself like a paper bag. "Help!" he shouted. "It's a fox killer! It's a dangerous dagger-toothed slaughterer! Get me out of here!"

Just then, a truck roared into the farmyard and two yellow lights beamed through the darkness. "It's Mr Cartwright!" said Hector. "We're saved!"

Mr Cartwright climbed out of his truck. "Blow me down!" he said, clumping across the yard. "It's the fox! Get out of here, you beast!" He shone his torch into the field, lighting up Finlay's bushy tail as it disappeared into the hedge never to return to the farm again.

Mr Cartwright took off his cap and wiped his forehead. "Phew! That was close." Then he noticed Hector standing in the field, surrounded by all the hens. "Hector, what are you doing here? Did you scare that fox?"

Hector trailed his hoof through the mud, feeling awkward. "Yes I did," he thought. "Aren't I brave? Aren't you proud of me, Mr Cartwright?"

The hens bustled round Hector, clucking and squawking. "Oh, thank you, Hector!" cried the smallest hen. "You showed that fox! You saved us all!"

Mr Cartwright waded through the chickens and patted Hector on the nose. "Sorry I'm late, everyone. The traffic was a nightmare." He pulled an apple from his pocket and gave it to Hector. "I don't know how you got here, my boy," he said. "Did you break out of your stable? Good job you did, though – seems you saved the day!"

Hector's Hens

He started shooing the hens towards their coop. "Come on, girls, bedtime now... hang on a minute." He stared as Hector followed the chickens into their warm shed and lay down. Mr Cartwright rubbed his eyes. "You can't fit in there, boy."

"I think I can, Mr Cartwright," thought Hector as he munched the apple and snuggled into the hay.

The farmer shook his head and laughed. "Go on then. I don't suppose it will do any harm for just one night."

As Mr Cartwright was about to walk away, he saw the damage to the hen house caused by Hector's crash landing and immediately understood what had happened. "You keep those hens nice and safe, Hector," he smiled, patting the horse gratefully on the head.

Hector closed his eyes. "One night? I don't think so. I saved the day, remember? I'm the Hen Hero and I'm staying here forever. Me and my hens. Hector's Hens." And he drifted off to sleep with the chickens roosting quietly around him on their perches.

Breaktime Bother

Archie sat on the playground bench, his knees drawn up to his chin. Noise blasted his ears from all directions: high squeaking screams, low rumbling roars and a general drone of jumbled chatter. Archie could never make out any actual words. He flinched at the rapid snap-clack-snap of the skipping ropes nearby and winced as a football slammed into the fence beside him making it – and Archie's world – wobble.

He stared miserably at the teacher, Ms Waffle, who was chatting to a group of children. "Blow the whistle!" Archie said to himself. "Just blow it! Tell me it's *In-time*. Please!"

But Ms Waffle spotted an argument between two girls right in the centre of the playground and headed towards it. Archie thought she was magic, the way she glided through the running, screaming children. Did she have an invisible shield round her, preventing any injury? How else did she just cut through the chaos without getting bumped or trodden on, hit with a ball or blasted with noise?

Archie had been bumped many times during his first week in the Big Playground. Now that he was six, he was 'old enough' to leave the safe Small Playground. How he missed that comforting enclosed space with its softly springy tarmac and smiling painted animals.

On the first day in the Big Playground, his classmates had raced out of the stuffy building, shrieking with excitement and charging up and down the wide open space. Archie copied the other children but within moments a Year Five boy had kicked a soft ball into Archie's face. "Ooops sorry," the boy had said, crouching down so his flushed face was level with Archie's. "Are you OK?"

Archie had brushed the bubble of water from his eyes and pretended he was fine. *It's only a soft ball*, he'd said to himself. *They don't really hurt.* But it did hurt and he had a red smudge on his nose to prove it. It didn't matter that it had disappeared by lunchtime –

he remembered the pain.

Things only got worse when, the next day, a Year Four girl had trodden on his foot as she played *Jump Up and Down a Lot* with some other girls. Again, the girl had stopped and apologised, her eyes wide and concerned, but Archie had sniffed and hobbled to the edge of the playground. He'd climbed onto a stripy red and blue seat and waited for playtime to finish. Before long, this brightly painted bench was to become 'his' bench.

Over the next few weeks, Archie's classmates seemed to learn the rules. They managed to dodge footballs, avoid flying skipping ropes and swerve spinning hoops. They found a way to weave in and out of the Big Children games like the mysterious *Run and Shout* and the unfathomable *Spaceman-Football-Hunter-Chase*. But Archie failed to grasp these new games with their ever-changing rules. It didn't matter where he stood, someone or something clonked him over the head, or brushed his arm or simply made him jump with surprise. After a while, he decided playtimes were just frightening and

Breaktime Bother

his only option was to sit on the bench, hiding behind his knees.

"Why don't you play with us, Archie?" Freya had asked one breaktime. She and Archie had spent ages making salt-dough mini-beasts in the classroom. They'd had wings and wiggly feelers and Freya had laughed so much at Archie's *Wobbly Worm* voice, she'd started hiccupping. But now that they were outside, in the 'Battleground' as Archie called thought of it, he had no time for Freya or Ross or Mikey. All his classroom friends had the Special Power. They knew how to survive in the 'Battleground'. And Archie didn't.

One lunchtime when Archie thought it would never, ever be *In-time*, he noticed a tall girl wandering towards him. He recognised her as Molly, from one of the Year Five classes. She sometimes came into their room to read with the younger children.

"Hey, Archie?" she said, sitting next to him. "I saw you here yesterday. Haven't you got anyone to play with?"

Archie felt his insides crumple with embarrassment and he dug his face into his knees and hid.

Molly nudged his arm. "What about those two over there?" she pointed at Freya and Mikey who were playing *Chase the Dinosaur*. "Aren't they your friends?"

Archie lifted his head up, annoyed with her ignorance. "I've got lots of friends," he snapped. "I just don't like playing."

Molly looked surprised. "Really?"

"I mean, I do like playing, I just…" Now he felt even more stupid. He'd have to admit that he was frightened. "I just… I just…"

"Oh, I get it!" Molly jumped in. "Did you get bashed by the big children?"

Archie nodded, his ears suddenly red hot. No point pretending.

Molly pulled a bag of crisps from her coat pocket and offered one to Archie. "Cheese and onion."

Archie didn't really like cheese and onion but he felt he shouldn't say no. He took a crisp, said thank you, and stared at Molly. She looked strong and grown up and like nothing could ever worry her. Archie knew she could read every single word that ever existed in the world because she would read any book the class picked for her – the whole way through – without even stopping. He guessed she knew all the rules to the games in the playground. He'd seen her playing lots of them. He focused on the wispy bits of her hair that had escaped from under the yellow bobble hat she wore. He didn't want to cry. He was trying so hard, he didn't realise she'd spoken.

"Pardon?" he said, chewing on the oniony crisp. He knew he'd still be able to taste it when he was at home watching *Terror Pterodactyl TV.*

"I said that I used to be scared too. People bumped into me. And once, a skipping rope—"

"*You* were?" Archie couldn't believe someone like Molly could ever be scared. "You were scared?"

Molly laughed. "Yes! I was little once, like you. Took me ages to get used to it out here."

Archie stared. He shook his head. Nope. This grown-up wondergirl was never small. Never!

Molly suddenly crushed her crisp packet. "Right. We're going over to the bin. I need to throw this away."

Archie held back. "But it's over there." He pointed through the swaying throng of children. "I'll have to walk round the edge."

"Come with me." Molly started walking and Archie followed. He trusted Molly. She was kind and seemed to shower him with sparkles of confidence.

Keeping his eyes on the fluffy bobble of Molly's hat, Archie followed her into the centre of the playground. A crowd of children swarmed towards him, chasing a football as it skimmed past his toes.

Aaah! He flung his arms over his head and, without waiting for Molly, he sprinted back to the bench. *It's no good*, he thought, sinking into his coat. *I just can't do it.*

"What happened to you?" It was Molly, standing over him with her arms folded. "I turned round and you'd disappeared!"

"There were hundreds of people, all chasing me and running at me," Archie quivered.

Molly frowned. "Are you sure about that?" she said.

"Erm…" Archie stared at a pigeon flying

over the playground. "They might have been chasing a ball."

"*Hundreds* of people?" Molly repeated.

Once again, Archie felt his ears getting hot. "Well…" he chewed the inside of his cheek. "Maybe there weren't hundreds…"

"Of course there weren't," Molly grabbed his sleeve. "Come on. You just have to get used to it. People don't want to hurt you."

She tried to make him move, but he ran behind the bench and squeezed into the gap between the seat and the school fence. He was about to tell her to go away when the whistle blew. Ah, that sweet sound. How he loved that squeaky shriek!

In-time! It was *in-time!*

The next day, Archie sat on his bench and found himself looking for Molly and her yellow bobble hat. That bobble was quite friendly, wasn't it? How could a piece of fluffy wool be friendly? He didn't know, but for some reason the sight of the wobbly pom-pom made him feel safe. Today he felt cold though, and a little bit sad. Molly had been trying to help him and all he did was run back here, to his bench. He hated this bench. *When I'm grown up,* he said to himself, *I'm never going to sit on a bench ever again, even if I've walked a hundred miles – I'll sit on the floor.*

"What are you thinking about, Dreamy Head?"

Archie looked up in surprise. It was Molly! She'd come over to him again. He was very pleased.

"Molly," he said, quickly. "I'm sorry I—"

"Come on." Molly laid a piece of orange paper on the ground just in front of his feet. "I've made dinosaur footprints," she said, standing on the card. It was a bit longer than her foot and had three spiky bits, like claws. Archie thought it was a very good dinosaur footprint and he wished he could make one.

"I've made loads!" said Molly holding out her hands. "We have to follow them… Quick!"

A delicious giggle burst from Archie's mouth and he sat up, peering across the playground. He loved dinosaurs! Sure enough, there amongst the mass of feet and legs, footballs and hoops, he could see patches of orange. There was one behind the netball post,

another in front of the PE shed and one by the gate into the field. Molly had put them all over the place!

She was already heading towards the first footprint, which was near a group of boys having skipping races. Archie focused on the dinosaur footprints. He set off after her, his heart beating wildly.

At first, he moved slowly, creeping past children with his shoulders tense and his arms tight by his side. But he kept his eyes on Molly's friendly bobble hat, knowing she was there in front of him. Once he reached the first footprint, he realised he hadn't been bumped. He also realised people were moving, stepping aside for him. No one had knocked into him.

He knelt down to get the footprint and Molly shouted behind him. "That's the first one, now come and get the others!"

He spun round and chased after her, excitement helping him find a path through the other children.

"It's here! Look!" Molly was leaning up against the PE shed, pointing at the tarmac. "See? The Leaf-eating Leafosaurus, it's been waiting for us to find it!"

Archie followed her outstretched hand. Of course there was nothing there apart from the wire fence, but the more Molly described Leafosaurus, the more he pictured it.

"She loves big, juicy plants. I've just given her a handful," said Molly, scooping up some brown leaves from the ground. "And look at her long neck! That's how she gets the tall trees."

Arche giggled and found more leaves.

Molly clapped her hands and darted back into the crowd. "Let's find another dinosaur!

Follow me!"

Archie ran after her. *I'll find the next one*, he thought. *I'm going to be first!* He charged across the playground, roaring at the top of his voice. For some reason, he'd decided he was the dinosaur and Molly was going to have to catch him. He felt his strong, scaly feet and claws scraping the earth. He stretched his long, bendy neck and sniffed out the tallest trees. "ROOOAR!" he said.

"Hey, Archie, what are you playing?" It was Freya, looking up at him with a grin. "It sounds really fun."

Archie stopped roaring. "Erm... I'm a Leafosaurus. I'm looking for leaves."

Mikey appeared behind Freya. "Can I play?"

"Yeah, me too?" said Freya.

Archie glanced at Molly who was heading towards a footprint by the gate. *Would she mind?* Somehow he knew she wouldn't mind at all. He turned to his friends. "Of course you can. We have to follow the footprints and one of you can be a different dinosaur."

"Whoop!" shouted Freya galloping towards the PE shed.

"YES!" roared Mikey.

Archie never found the playground scary again. Each morning he saw Molly and sometimes she invented a new game. Sometimes she played with him and his friends and other times she went off with other friends. There were occasions when he got a small bump from a football or a knock from another child rushing by, but it didn't happen very often.

In the next few years, Archie grew to be one of the tallest boys in the school. He still liked to play dinosaurs and he loved running round the playground, tearing up and down, chasing his friends. He enjoyed football, hula-hooping and he was particularly good at skipping. One day, he caught sight of a boy sitting on the bench by the school gate. He'd stopped calling it 'his' bench ages ago, but seeing the way the boy hugged his knees sent Archie right back to being six again.

He put his skipping rope in the box and wandered over to the boy. "Hello!" he said, perching on the seat. Funny how it now felt like a small bench instead of something he needed a step to climb on.

The boy kept his arms clasped round his legs, his tiny feet resting on the edge of the bench. Archie stared at the playground with the flurry of playtime fun. He sat back and remembered how it had seemed: wild, dangerous, unpredictable and frightening.

WHOOSH! A football whizzed past, just missing the boy's head. He whimpered and buried his face in his hands.

"Hey," Archie edged a little closer. "I know it's scary, but it will be OK, I promise."

The boy turned to stare. "What?" He had huge brown eyes, overflowing with tears.

"I mean," Archie tried to think of something to say. "I was scared too when I was your age."

Breaktime Bother

"You were?" The boy looked as if Archie had told him he was an alien.

Archie nodded. "Yeah. I couldn't even walk across the playground without crying. It's OK, you get used to it."

The boy folded his arms and stuck his lower lip out. "I'll never get used to it. I want to go back to the Small Playground."

"Trust me," Archie pointed towards the PE shed on the opposite side of the playground. "If you look over there, you'll see something amazing."

"Really?" The boy's eyes widened. "What do you mean, amazing?"

"Well…" Archie leaned back on the seat, his body far too big for it, and waited for an idea to form in his head. At last he glanced at the small boy. "Have you ever seen a dinosaur footprint?"

The Ice Mice

The farm lay under a thick blanket of snow. Icicles hung off trees, sparkling in the sunlight, while frost glinted on the frozen puddles that were scattered across the yard like fallen frisbees. At the edge of the farmyard, Flossie Mouse crept into the sunshine, blinking at the dazzling scene.

"Gosh!" she exclaimed. "Everything's so different." She glanced behind her and giggled, seeing the tiny tracks she'd made in the snow. They looked like a trail of little insects following her across the grass.

"Come on, Flossie!" It was her sister, Nancy, already scampering ahead. "Let's go ice skating! Race you to the cattle trough!"

Nancy scurried up the sides of the giant metal tank, but Flossie hesitated. She knew they weren't supposed to go on the ice. Mum and Dad had told them so many times about the dangers. But Nancy stood at the top now, reaching her paws out, her eyes shining. "Flossie, hurry up!" she squeaked. "Last one to the end of the trough is a smelly cat!"

Flossie felt as if her tummy was full of grasshoppers. How she longed to join her sister up there! She tiptoed closer and began to scramble up the steep edges. When she reached her sister, she slapped a paw over her mouth, gazing at the glistening, smooth surface of the tank. "Golly gosh!" she exclaimed. "It looks like a magical wonderland!"

"And it's wonderfully slippery!" said Nancy, gliding on one leg into the middle of the ice.

Flossie clung to the metal rim with all four paws. "Mum said never—"

"That's only if it gets warmer," shouted Nancy, switching to a different leg. "And it's freezing today, isn't it? Brrrrrrrr!" She skidded to a halt, sending an arc of ice over her sister. "I'll look after you, don't worry, Floss."

Flossie shrieked and giggled under the cold shower. If Nancy said it was safe, then it must be. Shaking ice from her whiskers, she stepped onto the solid surface. "Race you to that tree!"

The tree grew next to the trough, where one

leafless branch trailed low, scraping the ice of the trough. Flossie had noticed it when she was on the ground, thinking it would make an excellent climbing frame. Now that she was up on the top, though, it seemed the tree was an awfully long way away.

"OOOH!" she wobbled for a few moments, her tiny paws slipping and sliding from under her. "I'm not sure I can do this."

Nancy glided past and grabbed Flossie's tail. "It's OK, just follow me. You'll soon get the hang of it."

After a few more stumbles, thuds and forward rolls, Flossie began to get used to the feel of the ice under her feet. Before long, she was gliding and spinning with her sister and laughing with joy.

"You've got it!" called Nancy, twirling on the spot.

Time flew by – and so did the mice! – racing each other, looping, gliding and spinning. "Wheeeeee!" they shrieked, speeding faster and faster, their ears pinned back and their fur ruffled up in the breeze.

After a while, they sat on the tree branches

for a rest. Flossie gazed across the field where the cows stood in the yard, cloudy puffs of hot breath hovering over their noses. The farmer appeared, stamping her feet and blowing on her hands. "Morning, my lovelies," she said, greeting each cow with a tap on the back. "You all ready for your breakfast?" She opened the gate and the cows wandered slowly into the field, their hooves unsteady on the fresh snow. The farmer jogged in front of them, singing loudly as she tossed armfuls of hay for them.

Up on the water trough, Flossie's ears began to tingle. "What lovely singing," she whispered. "Makes me want to dance."

"It is rather pretty," agreed Nancy.

Flossie lifted a paw and tapped it against the ice. "Do you think we could...?"

"Could what?" said Nancy, smiling.

"Dance?"

"Ooh! *Yes!* Come on!"

Arm in arm, the sisters whirled across the ice, leaving a trail of slithery patterns that snaked and curled like worms. Flossie felt the farmer's singing carrying her. It powered her movements, taking control of her legs.

"Twirl to the left," she said to Nancy. "And now to the right. Join tails together whilst spinning on our toes…"

Nancy copied Flossie's moves, each action merging into the other. It happened so smoothly, that before they'd even got to the edge of the trough, they had invented an entire dance!

"I've had another idea," said Flossie. "I think we could try skating backwards… Oh!" She slammed into her sister who had suddenly stopped. "What's the matter?"

The Ice Mice

A large grey nose had appeared on the edge of the water trough. Flossie backed away, trembling. The nose belonged to a brown-eyed cow!

"Hello," said the cow. "I was looking for a drink, but the water's not here – just this cold stuff."

"It's frozen at the moment," said Flossie. "I hope you don't mind us using your trough for skating?"

The cow shook her head. "I don't mind at all. In fact I've been watching you for a while and your dancing is the most beautiful thing I've ever seen."

Flossie and Nancy hugged each other, giggling. "Really?" said Flossie, "I mean, we've only just started practising – it will be much better once we work out all the moves."

"I think it's wonderful already." The cow blinked her long eyelashes. "I'm Marigold, by the way. Please dance some more. Please."

The two mice bowed then curtseyed, nodded to each other and then cleared their throats. "Erm… Welcome to our dance," said Flossie, shyly. "It's called… er…"

"The *Ice Mice*!" cheered Nancy.

And so they danced. Marigold stared with wide-eyed wonder, her head following the graceful movement of the twirling mice. Flossie felt like a bird, like she could soar into the sky, like she could touch the clouds, like she—

CRACK!

A terrible wrenching sound knocked Flossie off her feet. With an ear-splitting roar, a gap appeared in the ice – a wide, gaping hole, like a huge mouth! Flossie screamed and tried to scramble to the edge, but the gap began to spread, reaching towards her until...

"*Aaaaaargh!*" The ice collapsed, crashing into the freezing water. Flossie leaped for the side of the trough, desperate to avoid the hole. "*Nooooo!*" She watched in terror, her heart splintering into thousands of pieces as Nancy fell, disappearing into the cold darkness.

"*Help!*" Flossie clawed at the slippery sides, but it was no good. Within seconds she too felt herself falling, and everything went dark.

Water filled her ears, her nose and her mouth. It froze every muscle, every whisker.

The Ice Mice

She tried to swim, beating the water with her paws, but chunks of ice bumped her face, knocking her sideways. Her chest began to hurt and she knew she would have to take a breath soon, but the top of the trough seemed so far away. *Where's Nancy?* she thought. *Now we'll never get to perform, we'll never show Mum and Dad our beautiful dance. Oh, if only we hadn't gone on the ice!*

Flossie's thoughts faded as something nudged her back. At first she thought it was another ice chunk, but there it was again, a gentle prodding feeling, soft and warm... *warm?* Flossie's brain struggled to focus as the soft thing lifted her, pushing her up through the water, out of the darkness and into the light.

"Blurgh!" Flossie coughed, gulping air into her lungs again. She reached out a paw. Thank goodness – she was on firm ground, in a clump of dry hay. She forced her eyes open and stared straight into a pair of wide, brown eyes, fringed with long lashes. "Marigold? Is that you?"

Marigold mooed softly, breathing warm

air on Flossie's fur. "Yes, are you OK, little mouse?"

Flossie sat up. "I am now, but where's Nancy?"

"I'm here, Floss," said Nancy, wringing water from her ears. "I'm right beside you. Thanks to Marigold."

"Oh!" Flossie hugged her sister and sobbed. "I was so scared. I thought I was drowning and then... Marigold!" She glanced up. "You saved us, Marigold! That was your nose helping me out of the water! How can we ever thank you enough?"

Marigold scraped her hoof in the snow. "It was nothing really." She was already nosing the pile of hay with interest. Flossie clung to her sister. "We should *never* have gone on that ice, Nancy."

"I know," Nancy nodded. "Who'd have thought it could break as quickly as that? It mustn't have been as thick as we thought."

"I think I'll make a sign," said Flossie, "to warn everyone about the dangers of walking on frozen ponds, or... water troughs."

"Good idea," said Marigold, chewing a

mouthful of hay. "Shame, though, I did so love your dancing. You two are enchanting!"

"It was rather special, wasn't it? I felt like a fairy-angel-mouse!" Flossie sighed. "But we can still dance, can't we? We don't have to be on ice!" She prodded the hard ground. "Just imagine the wonderful dances we can invent on dry land."

"Brilliant!" said Nancy. "Instead of Ice Mice, we'll be Mice Dancers!"

"That's wonderful," said Marigold. "I can't wait to watch you. Now, if you don't mind, I'm going to have a drink of water. Someone's broken the ice at last!"

Tilly the Tooth Fairy

Tilly peered in the window of the bedroom. Good. As moonlight filled the room she could see that Henry seemed to be fast asleep in the top bunk – though it was difficult to get a proper look for the little boy was surrounded with cuddly toys! His younger brother, Leo, was also sleeping soundly in the bunk underneath, his hand clutching a cuddly toy zebra that looked as though it was very well-loved indeed.

Tilly smiled and quickly slipped between the narrow gap left by the slightly open window, and flew down to Leo's bed. Delicately she felt under his pillow. Where was his tooth? Unfortunately his head was pressing right on the edge of his pillow and she couldn't get her tiny hands very far under it. She sighed as she felt around. She couldn't find the tooth anywhere! But she knew that one of his teeth had come out today. The tooth fairy network was never wrong.

She darted over to the other side of the bed, her delicate wings causing the slightest breeze as she flew over Leo's face, but he didn't stir. Quickly, she felt under the pillow again, and carefully, so as not to wake the sleeping boy, her fingers worked their way further and further under the pillow. Suddenly, Leo turned his head and opened his eyes. Quick as a flash, Tilly pulled out her hand and flitted out of sight.

The little fairy waited breathlessly. Had he seen her? No. There was no cry, no sound of movement and soon she heard Leo's deep breathing as he drifted back to sleep. Once she was sure it was safe, she flew back to her task. At least he had moved his head now. Her hand slipped easily under the pillow and her fingers finally found the small tooth. She pulled it out from under the pillow, replaced it with a silver coin and then quickly flew out of the window.

Phew! That had been close – it was a matter of pride to her that no child had ever seen her collecting their teeth. That was the last collection of the night, too. Just as well because the sun was starting to rise and the sky was beginning to brighten. Tilly made her flight back to Fairy Palace. She was ready for breakfast!

As she flew, Tilly was thinking of all the delicious things she might have for breakfast – cereal or scrambled eggs, or toast with loads of honey – when she heard crying coming from somewhere below her. She looked around and flew down to the treetops. There she saw Aidan, one of her best friends, sobbing his heart out. Tilly quickly settled beside him and put her arm around the sad fairy.

"Oh, Aidan, what's wrong?" Tilly asked her friend.

"I've failed everyone!" Aidan whispered, tearfully and then he started to cough.

"I'm sure you haven't!" Tilly said.

"I have!" sobbed Aidan, holding up his money bag. "Look how much I've got left!"

Tilly looked inside the bag. It held quite a few coins. "Have you forgotten to leave the coins for the teeth you've collected?" she asked.

Aidan started coughing again. "No," he

wailed. "I've only collected half the teeth on my list for tonight!"

"Why? What happened?" asked Tilly.

"It's this cough," Aidan explained. "I was in the middle of collecting a tooth when it started. I made such a noise, the little girl woke up."

"Oh, no!" gasped Tilly. "Did she see you?"

Aidan shook his head. "No. I flew straight out of the window. I coughed so much when I got outside, I didn't dare go back after that," said Aidan, wiping his eyes. "I haven't visited anyone else because I was so worried I would start coughing again. But now there'll be children who will wake up today disappointed to find that their teeth haven't been collected."

"Well, we can't have that!" said Tilly. "Pass me your list. I will do it for you."

"But it's getting light!" Aidan protested.

"It's still early. Most children won't be waking up just yet. I'll be careful," Tilly reassured him. "I'm sure I can do it. You go home."

"But what will the fairy queen say?" asked Aidan. "She will be very cross."

"She won't know!" said Tilly. "Here, take my teeth and money bag and just drop them off as though they're yours. Then go to bed. You need to get warm and have a good sleep!"

Aidan gratefully took the things from Tilly and flew home. Tilly's stomach rumbled as she checked Aidan's list. She'd have to have scrambled egg, cereal *and* toast when she got back!

Fortunately, all of the children still to visit lived close together and their teeth were easy to find under their pillows. They all slept on as Tilly swapped her coins for their teeth and she was soon on her way home.

She arrived back at Fairy Palace just in time for breakfast and gobbled down a large helping of scrambled eggs, toast and cereal before going straight to bed.

The next evening, Tilly went to see Aidan. He was still in bed, coughing and sneezing and looking very poorly. "You poor thing. How are you feeling?"

"Oh, not too bad," croaked Aidan, but then he had a big coughing fit.

"Well, you're not going out tonight!" Tilly told him, firmly. "You can't! If you start coughing, you won't just wake the children, you'll wake the whole house!"

"But I can't miss my collections again! I've missed so many this year being unwell."

"We won't tell anyone," said Tilly. "Nights are long and dark at the moment, and it's a cloudy evening so nightfall will come even sooner. Children will have no trouble getting off to sleep as soon as they go to bed tonight. I will set off early and do your collections and mine, no trouble at all."

"Are you sure?" asked Aidan.

"Yes!" Tilly smiled. And off she flew.

Night after night, for almost a week, Tilly helped her friend. But doing double collections wasn't easy. Tilly was as quick as she could be, but some of her deliveries were difficult: one tooth had fallen under the bed, another just wasn't there no matter how hard she searched, and in a third house there was a spaniel asleep on the bedroom floor. Dogs were always a problem. They could sense her presence better than humans. Tilly had to be especially careful not to disturb them.

Tilly worked as hard and as fast as she could. But by the fourth night, she was beginning to tire and before she knew it, the night was over and dawn was breaking. When she saw that her next child was up and already playing with his toys, she knew she had to stop. She saw him suddenly look excitedly under his pillow. When he saw that his tooth was still there, he burst into tears.

Tilly felt awful. She had never, *ever* disappointed a child before. She wanted to fly in and give him his coin for his tooth, but of course she couldn't. Tooth Fairies must never be seen. She looked at her list again; she had four visits still to make, but it was impossible. The children were already awake. Tilly could only hope that they wouldn't check their pillows until she came again the following night. She would have to make sure she visited them first.

When she returned to Fairy Palace, the fairy queen was waiting for her, and she looked cross.

"You're very late, Tilly. What happened?"

"I'm sorry, Your Majesty," said Tilly. "Some of the teeth were difficult to find. And, um, well, I got a bit lost..." Tilly felt really bad about lying to the fairy queen, but she wanted to protect Aidan.

"Have you been wasting time, playing with their toys?" The fairy queen gave her a disapproving glare.

"No! Of course not!" Tilly protested. She knew some fairies did that but she never had. Fortunately, the fairy queen seemed to believe her.

"Well, you'd better have your breakfast quickly," said the queen. "It won't surprise you to see there isn't much left now."

The fairy queen was right. There were just two pieces of cold toast left on a plate and no honey at all. Still, that was better than nothing. She spread them with butter and ate them quickly before going to look in on Aidan. Tilly yawned. She was very tired after doing all those extra collections but she looked in on her friend before she went to bed.

"How did you get on?" Aidan asked her.

"Fine," said Tilly, wearily. It was another lie. "Are you feeling any better?"

"Much!" said Aidan, but he didn't sound any better. His nose was red from all the sneezing and blowing, and his voice sounded scratchy. Tilly pulled a face. She wasn't the only one being untruthful.

Tilly lay in bed unable to sleep. Every time she closed her eyes, she could picture the little boy crying with disappointment because she hadn't taken his tooth. Had he been sad all morning? Was his belief in tooth fairies destroyed forever?

Suddenly, Tilly had an idea. She rushed to the craft cupboard and found some tissue paper. She would make lots of paper fairies and give them to the children she'd had to disappoint as well as giving them their silver coins.

It was very late when she finished making the paper fairies and she barely had two hours' sleep before it was time to leave. She tiptoed to Aidan's room and found him sleeping – good! She left a note telling him that she was doing his collection again and picked up Aidan's list and bag of coins. Then, clutching her own things and the paper fairy gifts she'd made, she quickly flew off to do all the rounds. With yesterday's list to finish off, as well as a double load of new visits, she had a lot to do!

Tilly flew faster than ever. First, she went to the children whose teeth she had missed the night before and left them their money and paper fairies. Then she started on the new rounds. Maybe it was because she was flying at double speed, or because she'd been up late making the special gifts, but Tilly soon grew very tired. She kept on – she had no choice. She'd almost finished when she flew into a room belonging to a little boy called Logan. As she sat on his quilt, reaching under his pillow, she couldn't help thinking how wonderfully soft it was...

Tilly the Tooth Fairy

Tilly woke with a jolt as a sudden movement sent her tumbling off the bed. She just managed to stop herself calling out in surprise. Logan was waking up. Tilly must have fallen asleep right next to him on his lovely soft quilt. How long had she been there? Tilly glanced up at his clock. It was 7:15 am! She'd been there for nearly half an hour!

Fortunately, Logan had snuggled back down to sleep again. Tilly quickly flew up, felt under his pillow, replaced his tooth with a coin and flew away, just as his alarm clock rang. That was close!

Tilly checked her list again. She still had two more children to visit. She would have to leave them until tomorrow night.

After a week of double collections and sleepless days, Tilly was exhausted and it took her such a long time to fly back to Fairy Palace. She was so late she knew breakfast would be long over. As she tiptoed into the kitchen, hoping to find a leftover bread roll, she became aware of someone standing behind her.

"Tilly!"

Tilly jumped and dropped the bread roll on the floor. She turned to see the fairy queen.

"I know just what you've been up to!" said the fairy queen, frowning. "I found Aidan asleep in bed hours ago and I read your note. Have you collected all the teeth on both lists tonight?"

Tilly couldn't bring herself to lie to the fairy queen again. "Um, no, Your Majesty," she said, sorrowfully.

"Oh, Tilly!" said the fairy queen.

Tilly thought of the children who might be disappointed because their teeth hadn't been collected, and felt like crying too.

"It isn't a crime to be ill. Fairies get sick and need time to rest and recover until they are better. Do you see that, Tilly?"

"I do now, Your Majesty," said Tilly. "But Aidan was worried about getting into trouble because he'd been ill so many times before."

"Fairies only get into trouble when they *pretend* to be ill, " said the fairy queen. "But when they are really poorly, we all want to help them, not punish them. Fairies are kind and considerate, Tilly. No one gets into trouble if they are really ill."

Tilly hung her head in shame. "I didn't like to think of all the disappointed children who wouldn't get their tooth fairy coin, so I tried to do all Aidan's visits for him, and, well, it all became too much for me. I couldn't do all of his as well as mine. I'm sorry I lied to you."

Tilly started to cry. She felt so stupid – and exhausted.

"Now then, don't cry, Tilly," said the queen softly. "Come along, let's get you tucked up in bed."

Tilly didn't have the energy to protest. And before she knew it, she was snuggled up in bed, warm and cosy and fast asleep. She slept and slept and slept.

When Tilly awoke it was the middle of the night. "Oh no!" she cried, jumping out of bed. "I'm so late!"

But in the corner of the room, like any caring mother would, sat the fairy queen.

"Never mind that," she smiled warmly. "Go back to sleep. Aidan is recovered now thanks to your help, and he and the other fairies are sharing your work while you rest."

Tilly was still exhausted and tears began to fall again. "I just got completely overwhelmed," she said to the fairy queen.

Again, the fairy queen smiled a friendly smile and said, "When you feel overwhelmed and that things are too much for you, what should you do, Tilly?"

"I don't know!" said Tilly, shaking her head.

"You should ask for help," said the fairy queen. "Always! If anything is ever wrong, no matter what it is, you mustn't bottle it up inside you. If only you'd have told us before, we'd have all helped to share in doing Aidan's tooth collections."

"And then no children would have been disappointed," said Tilly.

"That's right," said the fairy queen, "but more importantly, you wouldn't have worn yourself out."

"I'm so sorry," said Tilly.

"Never mind that now," said the fairy queen. "You are a very kind fairy, Tilly."

The next morning, as all the other fairies returned to Fairy Palace, Tilly awoke and joined them for a breakfast feast where she

thanked them for helping with her collection.

The fairy queen spoke kindly to them all. "Thank you all for working together to help Tilly last night. She has shown herself to be a very kind friend. But we can't help others if we're ill, so we must remember to look after ourselves, too. And ask for help when we need it." The queen served everyone a special chocolate pastry as a treat.

"I might need some help finishing this!" Tilly winked to her friends as they tucked into their breakfast feast.

The Storyteller

Jake sat at the front of the class sulking. Just before school that morning, Mum had told him that his granny was coming to stay for the weekend. Jake dreaded Granny's visits. He thought they were so boring. She spent a lot of time napping, Jake wasn't allowed on his computer and, instead, was expected to sit and talk to his granny – and he could never think of anything to talk to her about. Jake stared at his teacher, Mr Grey. It was a good name for him because he always wore grey suits, grey shoes and grey ties. Added to that, he was really boring – a bit like a visit from Granny on a rainy Sunday afternoon.

"Right, class. Tidy away quick and ready for story time," said Mr Grey. In classrooms around the country – the world even! – children would be excited at the mention of story time. But not in Jake's class. Mr Grey's droning voice could make even the most marvellous story dull.

When the children were tidy and settled, Mr Grey said, "We're very lucky because we have a special visitor for story time today." There was a ripple of whispers. Having a visitor in school was always exciting.

Slowly, the classroom door opened and an old lady hobbled in. She wore a long, hooded cloak, which was threaded with reds, greens and purples. Each colour shimmered and sparkled as she moved. Jake felt a strange prickly feeling down the back of his neck.

Mr Grey helped the lady to sit down and she pulled back her hood, revealing long, silver hair. Jake saw she had a wrinkled face with kind, laughing eyes.

"Good morning, children," she said, smiling. "My name is Mrs Oldfield. Thank you for inviting me into your school. I'm very excited because I've got a wonderful story to share with you."

The children nodded and looked around eagerly to see what book she would be reading. Jake liked to look at the pictures. But Mrs Oldfield had no book. Jake sank down in his chair in another disappointed sulk.

Mrs Oldfield pointed at the classroom windows. "Mr Grey, please would you close the blinds? Thank you."

The room was suddenly dark, but Mrs Oldfield lifted a candle from her bag and lit it with a long match. She closed her eyes and said in a mystical voice, "Everyone stare at the flame. All eyes on the flame."

At first, Jake could hear his classmates giggling. He tried not to laugh too. It was all very strange. But the candle's flame seemed to call out to him and he couldn't stop staring. It wasn't just a flame now – he could see shapes and moving figures inside the yellow glow and, what was that? Faces? Jake kept his gaze on the flickering light. *I feel so sleepy*, he thought as Mrs Oldfield's soft voice filled the room. *I really want to close my…*

Suddenly, Mrs Oldfield stopped talking and Jake jerked upright in his seat. "Wow! Where *are* we?"

It was the classroom – their classroom – but different. The windows and door were still in the same place, as was the walk-in cupboard,

but everything else had changed. Instead of the electronic screen at the front of the room, Jake could see a tall, thin blackboard covered in chalk marks. His table was now a wooden desk with a lift-up lid and a ridge to keep pens in. All the other desks were arranged in straight rows, lined up like soldiers.

"Look around, children," said Mrs Oldfield, speaking so quietly that Jake had to lean forwards. "What can you see?"

Jake blinked. Where was the book corner? The computers? The rows of plastic trays? Everything seemed to have disappeared. Jake shivered. The room was very cold.

He glanced across the room where a group of boys and girls sat drinking milk from small glass bottles. *Look at their clothes*, he thought. *So strange!*

The boys were wearing grey shorts – even though it was freezing – and thick, knee-length socks. The girls wore plain, grey dresses, also with knee-high socks. Each child was dressed in a woolly jumper, which looked heavy and itchy.

Jake glanced down at his bright blue

sweatshirt with the school logo embroidered on it. *I think our uniform's nicer*, he thought.

Just then, two of the girls in the knitted jumpers waved him over to where they were sitting. "Hello," they said, smiling. "How wonderful to see you!"

The first girl wore her hair in long plaits, tied at the end with green ribbons. "I'm Brenda. Welcome to our school." She sat down and pointed to her friend. "This is Anne."

Anne was as smiley as Brenda. "Hello," she whispered. "Ssh, listen. Our lesson's about to start."

At the front of the classroom, a stern-looking teacher stood and began to write sums on the chalkboard. "Copy these into your books. Silence, please," said the stern voice.

"Is this your maths lesson?" asked Jake. Anne and Brenda nodded and giggled as they mimed falling asleep.

Looking around the room, Jake couldn't see any helpful posters or displays, or any brightly coloured blocks or beads, like he had in his classroom to help with maths. Jake thought the girls did well to seem so chipper about having such a boring classroom and he was instantly thankful for his own.

"What's your favourite lesson?" whispered Brenda.

"I really like ICT."

"Icy what?" said Anne, giggling.

"ICT, it's computing," explained Jake.

Brenda frowned. "Oh, like in maths?"

"Oh…" Jake thought for a moment. "No, it's when we use computers… but…" He looked across at the dark cupboard where the laptop trolley was kept. "I guess you don't have any of those."

At that moment, a loud bell began to ring. It was so loud, the whole class jumped. "End of the day, everyone! Time to go home… Look at the flame, children, look at the flame…"

Without really meaning to, Jake gazed at the yellow light and his eyes began to feel heavy again.

"How was that, class?" Mr Grey asked.

Jake opened his eyes and blinked. They were back in their classroom! He glanced at Mrs Oldfield, who had taken off her hood.

"Crumbs!" said Jake, sitting back in his

chair in disbelief.

When Dad and Jake arrived home from school that day, Jake rushed straight to the computer. But to his dad's amazement, it wasn't to play games like usual.

"Look!" Jake waved his parents over to look at the screen. He'd searched 'schools in the olden days' and spent the next half an hour eagerly looking at grainy old photos from history.

The next day, the children were waiting excitedly for Mrs Oldfield's return. They sat bolt upright in their seats, in silence, as she lit the candle. As soon as Jake focused on the wobbling flame, he felt himself floating until... *Whoosh!*

Every day that week, Mrs Oldfield returned to tell them a story and the class were transported to a time when things were very different. They met Brenda and Anne again and walked home from school with them – miles it was and many of the class grumbled and groaned, so used to being driven home. But then Brenda began to dance and they all joined in, singing and dancing until, before

they knew it, they were outside Brenda's house.

Another time, they met Anne and helped her with her chores, cleaning and tidying the house – things they'd never dream of doing at home. But Anne made up games and the chores were soon all done in a flurry of fun. Jake discovered the toilet was outside and Anne's television was one of only a few in the town – and it only showed black-and-white pictures! Each time Mrs Oldfield visited, Jake's class were entranced by the amazing things they saw.

On Thursday afternoon, Dad met Jake at the school gates. He had a glum look on his face. "Sorry, Jake. We'll have to walk to the bus stop and catch the bus home. My car's in the garage being fixed."

"No worries, Dad," said Jake happily. "Let's just walk all the way home! People used to walk to and from school in the olden days, you know!" Dad looked at Jake bemused. He usually moaned if he had to walk anywhere.

Walking took much, much longer than their usual drive home, but Dad and Jake chatted the whole way home. Jake enjoyed it so much, he said he'd walk every day if they could.

When Friday arrived, Mr Grey didn't seem so grey. He'd started wearing colourful ties and Jake could see orange socks peeping out from his trouser legs. *Maybe Mr Grey's not so boring after all*, he thought.

"OK, class," said Mr Grey. "It's Mrs Oldfield's last day today. Let's give her an extra warm welcome."

The old lady shuffled into the room and Jake clung to the edge of his chair. *I wonder where we'll go this time*, he thought, jiggling his feet under the table.

Mrs Oldfield reached into her bag, but instead of a candle, she brought out a book. It was an exciting story about travelling in time and the children loved the colourful pictures. But Jake couldn't help being disappointed they hadn't visited Brenda and Anne again.

As the story came to a close, Mrs Oldfield said, "Well then, children. I hope you've enjoyed your visits to the past. I've certainly enjoyed showing you."

It was home time and the children thanked Mrs Oldfield before rushing out to their parents. Jake stayed behind.

"I've loved it so much," he said, the words tumbling out of him. "Seeing the old classroom and how Brenda and Anne had fun all the time – they even seemed to enjoy school, even without the computers."

"Indeed," Mrs Oldfield nodded. "They made the best of what they had, didn't they?"

Jake nodded. He looked around his classroom and at Mr Grey and thought about his home and all the things he had that Anne and Brenda didn't, and he *was* grateful.

"You're right. Thank you, Mrs Oldfield!" He gave her a big smile and ran out onto the playground to meet his mum.

Outside, Jake's mum stood nervously waiting to take him home.

"Granny's in the car," she said. "Now, Jake, please be on your best behav—"

But she didn't finish her sentence as Jake interrupted with a loud, "Granny!" and a big wave as he trotted over to the car.

"Granny," he said giving her a big hug. "I've got so much to ask you!" And to Mum's surprise, he chatted to Granny non-stop until it was time for her to leave on Sunday afternoon!